The
New
Policeman

KATE THOMPSON

Greenwillow Books
An Imprint of HarperCollinsPublishers

This book is a work of fiction. References to real people, events, establishments, organizations, or locales are intended only to provide a sense of authenticity, and are used to advance the fictional narrative. All other characters, and all incidents and dialogue, are drawn from the author's imagination and are not to be construed as real.

The New Policeman
Copyright © 2005 by Kate Thompson
First published in 2005 in Great Britain by The Bodley Head,
an imprint of Random House Children's Books.
First published in the United States in 2007 by Greenwillow Books.

The right of Kate Thompson to be identified
as the author of this work has been asserted by her.

The text of this book is set in 13-point Centaur.
Book design by Paul Zakris.
"The One That Was Lost" © JDC Publications Ltd.

Library of Congress Cataloging-in-Publication Data
Thompson, Kate, (date).
The new policeman / Kate Thompson
    p. cm.
"Greenwillow Books."
Summary: Irish teenager J.J. Liddy discovers that time is leaking from his world into Tír na n'Óg, the land of the fairies, and when he attempts to stop the leak he finds out a lot about his family history, the music that he loves, and a crime his great-grandfather may or may not have committed.
ISBN-13: 978-0-06-117427-8 (trade bdg.) ISBN-10: 0-06-117427-0 (trade bdg.)
ISBN-13: 978-0-06-117428-5 (lib. bdg.) ISBN-10: 0-06-117428-9 (lib. bdg.)
[1. Time and space—Fiction. 2. Fairies—Fiction. 3. Music—Fiction.
4. Ireland—Fiction.] I. Title.
PZ7.T3715965Ne 2007 [Fic]—dc22 2006008246

First American Edition 10 9 8 7 6 5 4 3 2 1

Greenwillow Books

PART ONE

J.J. Liddy and his best friend, Jimmy Dowling, often had arguments. J.J. never took them seriously. He even considered them a sign of the strength of the friendship, because they always made up again straightaway, unlike some of the girls in school, who got into major possessive battles with one another. But on that day in early September, during the first week that they were back in school, they had an argument like none before.

J.J. couldn't even remember now what it had been about. But at the end of it, at the point where they usually came round to forgiving each other and patching it up, Jimmy had dropped a bombshell.

"I should have had more sense than to hang around with you anyway, after what my granny told me about the Liddys."

His words were followed by a dreadful silence, full of J.J.'s bewilderment and Jimmy's embarrassment. He knew he had gone too far.

"What about the Liddys?" said J.J.

"Nothing." Jimmy turned to go back into school.

J.J. stood in front of him. "Go on. What did she tell you?"

Jimmy might have been able to wriggle his way out of it and pretend it was a bluff, but he had been overheard. He and J.J. were no longer alone. Two other lads, Aidan Currie and Mike Ford, had overheard and had come to join in.

"Go on, Jimmy," said Aidan. "You may as well tell him."

"Yeah," said Mike. "If he doesn't know he must be the only person in the county who doesn't."

The bell rang for the end of the morning break. They all ignored it.

"Know what?" said J.J. He felt cold, terrified, not of something that might happen but of something that he might find inside himself; in his blood.

"It was a long time ago," said Jimmy, still trying to retract.

"What was?"

"One of the Liddys . . ." Jimmy said something else but he mumbled it beneath his breath and J.J. couldn't hear. It sounded like "burgled the beast."

The teacher on yard duty was calling them in. Jimmy began to walk toward the school. The others fell in.

"He did what?" said J.J.

"Forget it," said Jimmy.

It was Aidan Currie who said it, loud enough for J.J. or anyone else to hear. "Sure, everyone knows about it. Your great-granddad. J.J. Liddy, same as yourself. He murdered the priest."

J.J. stopped in his tracks. "No way!"

"He did, so," said Mike. "And all for the sake of an old wooden flute."

"You're a shower of liars!" said J.J.

The boys, except for Jimmy, laughed.

"Always mad for the music, the same Liddys," said Mike.

He began to hop and skip toward the school in a goofy parody of Irish dancing. Aidan trotted beside him, singing an out-of-tune version of "The Irish Washerwoman." Jimmy glanced back at J.J. and, his head down, followed them as they went back in.

J.J. stood alone in the yard. It couldn't be true. But

he knew, now that he thought about it, that there had always been something behind the way some of the local people regarded him and his family. A lot of people in the community came to the céilís and the set-dancing classes that were held at his house on Saturdays. They had always come, and their parents and grandparents had come before them. In recent years the numbers had increased dramatically with the influx of new people into the area. Some of them came from thirty miles away and more. But there was, and always had been, a large number of local people who would have nothing to do with the Liddys or their music. They didn't exactly cross the street to avoid J.J. and his family, but they didn't talk to them either. J.J., if he'd thought about it at all, had assumed it was because his parents were one of the only couples in the district who weren't married, but what if that wasn't the reason? What if it had really happened? Could J.J. be descended from a murderer?

"Liddy!"

The teacher was standing at the door, waiting for him.

J.J. hesitated. For a moment it seemed to him that there was no way he could set foot inside that school again. Then the solution came to him.

The teacher closed the door behind him. "What do you think you were doing, standing out there like a lemon?"

"Sorry," said J.J. "I didn't realize you were talking to me."

"Who else would I be talking to?"

"My name's Byrne," said J.J. "My mother's name is Liddy all right, but my father's name is Byrne. I'm J.J. Byrne."

THE LEGACY

Trad

The new policeman stood on the street outside Green's pub. On the other side of the bolted doors a gathering of musicians was at full throttle, the rich blend of their instruments cutting through the bee-hive buzz of a dozen conversations. Across the road the rising tide slopped against the walls of the tiny harbor. Beneath invisible clouds the water was pewter gray with muddy bronze glints where it caught the street lights. Its surface was ragged. The breeze was getting up. There would be rain before long.

Inside the pub there was a momentary hiccup in the music as one tune ended and another began. For a couple of bars a solitary flute carried the new tune until the other musicians recognized it and pounced on it, and lifted it to the rafters of the old pub. Out in the street, Garda O'Dwyer recognized the tune. Inside his regulation black brogues his cramped toes twitched to the beat. At the curbside behind him his partner, Garda Treacy, leaned across the empty passenger seat of the squad car and tapped on the window.

Larry O'Dwyer sighed and took a step toward the narrow double doors. He'd had a good reason for becoming a policeman, but sometimes it was difficult to remember what it was. It wasn't this; he was sure of that much. He hadn't become a policeman to curtail the enjoyment of musicians and their audiences. A few miles away, in Galway city, violent crime was escalating dramatically. Street gangs were engaged in all kinds of thuggery and muggery. He would be of far more use to society there. But that, as far as he could remember, was not why he had become a policeman either. There were times, like now, when he suspected that the reason, whatever it was, might not have been a particularly good one.

The tune changed again. The light inside the squad car came on as Garda Treacy opened his door. Larry stilled his tapping foot and rapped with his knuckles on Mary Green's door.

Inside the pub throats closed, conversations

collapsed, the drone of voices faltered and died. One by one the musicians dropped out of the tune, leaving, for a while, an oblivious fiddler tearing away enthusiastically on her own. Someone got through to her finally, and the music stopped mid-bar. The only sound that followed was Mary Green's light footsteps crossing the concrete floor.

One of the narrow doors opened a crack. Mary's anxious face appeared. Behind her, Larry could see Anne Korff perched on a bar stool. She was one of the few people in the village that he had already met. He hoped he would not be required to take her name.

"I'm sorry, now," he said to Mary Green. "It's a quarter to one."

"They're just finishing up," said Mary earnestly. "They'll be gone in five minutes."

"I hope so," said Larry. "That would be the best thing for everyone."

As he returned to the car, the first drops of rain were beginning to fall onto the surface of the sea.

THE NEW POLICEMAN

Trad

They were falling, as well, on J.J. Liddy—or J.J. Byrne, as he now called himself. They were falling on his father, Ciaran, and on the last few bales of hay that they were loading on to the flatbed trailer in the Ring Field, the highest meadow on their land.

"How's that for timing?" said Ciaran.

J.J. didn't answer. He was too tired to answer. Inside his gloves his fingers were red raw from the hundreds of bale strings that had been through his hands that evening. He threw up the last bale. Ciaran stacked it neatly and dropped down into the tractor seat. J.J. helped Bosco up into the cab beside him. The dog was too old and stiff now to jump up on his own, but he wasn't too old to want to be part of everything that was happening on the farm. Wherever there was work being done, there was Bosco.

Ciaran let in the clutch and the old tractor began to rumble and clunk across the new-mown meadow. J.J. climbed up on top of the bales. The rain was falling more heavily now. Drops slanted across the headlight beam as they skirted the ring fort and emerged onto the rutted track that led down to the farmyard.

Ciaran was right. It was good timing. The hay they had just saved was a late crop, almost an afterthought. The summer had been wet, and their previous attempts at hay making had been disastrous. In the end they had brought in contractors to wrap what was left of their crop in round black bales. It had been too wet to be hay but not fresh enough to be silage. They called the resulting hybrid haylage, but it was optimistic. Even if the stock were hungry enough to eat it, they wouldn't get a great deal of nutrition from it. This crop was good, and it would make up some of the fodder shortfall, but by no means all of it. Farming was a tough station.

The trailer lurched. In the cab ahead of him, J.J. could see Bosco's tail waving about as he was thrown from side to side. To their right, on the other side of the electric fence, was Molly's Place, the field behind the house that the Liddys had called after some long-forgotten donkey. A stream of mottled shapes was moving across it now, like a school of fish gliding through the black depths of the sea. The goats— white Saanens and brown-and-white Toggenburgs— were heading for their shelter at the edge of the yard.

Goats hated rain. So did J.J. Now that he had stopped working, his body temperature had plummeted. Drops were rolling out of his hair and stinging his eyes. He longed for his bed.

Ciaran swung the tractor round in the yard. "We'll unload in the morning."

J.J. nodded, hopped down from the bales, and semaphored to Ciaran as he reversed the trailer into the empty bay of the hay shed. His mother, Helen, emerged from the back door and came over.

"Brilliant timing," she said. "Tea's just made."

But J.J. walked straight past the pot, which steamed on the range in the kitchen, and the plates of fresh scones on the table. Upstairs in his room, his school-bag lay open on his bed, leaking overdue homework. He glanced at the clock. If he got up half an hour early the next morning he could get a bit of it done.

He spilled the bag and its contents onto the floor, and as he set the alarm he wondered, as he wondered every day, where on earth all the time went.

THE NEW-MOWN
MEADOW

Trad

It wasn't that Mary Green didn't want her customers to leave. The bar was firmly closed and she had been pleading with them all to go since the new policeman had knocked. Most of her regulars had drunk up and gone, but not all. Some of the musicians were from out of town, and this was one of the best sessions they had played in years. Their fingers, their bows, their breath—the instruments themselves, it seemed—had all been taken over by the spirit of that wild, anarchic music. They wanted to oblige Mary, who was pacing the floor and wringing her hands in anxiety, but they just couldn't. Tunes they hadn't heard for years kept popping into their heads and demanding to be played. It was always like that in Green's. There was just something about the place.

It was 1:30 A.M. Outside in the street, Garda Larry O'Dwyer was standing in the pouring rain, paralyzed by the beauty of the music behind Mary's blackout curtains. But this time Garda Treacy was at his side and ready to go in.

"Bad luck to stop them in the middle of a tune," said Larry, but Treacy was already pounding on the door.

Mary opened it. "They're going," she said. "They're packed up and all."

The two guards edged past her just in time to catch a glimpse of a pair of heels and a fiddle case disappearing out of the back door. Larry knew he'd seen them before. He also knew how pointless it would be to try and remember where. Before anyone else could slip out the same way, Garda Treacy crossed the pub floor and stood beside the back door, taking out his notebook on the way. All the tables, even the ones surrounded by musicians, were clear and tidy. It was music, not drink, that had kept the crowd where they were. Nonetheless, they were all breaking the law.

Garda Treacy began to take the names of the musicians. Larry pulled out his notebook.

"There's no need," said Mary Green helplessly. "They're all going now."

Anne Korff was sitting where Larry had last seen her, on a bar stool beside the street door. He opened the notebook and took the lid off his pen.

"Name?"

"Er ... Lucy Campbell," said Anne Korff in a distinct German accent.

"Lucy Campbell," said Larry, fixing her with what he intended to be a hard stare.

She subdued the smile still wriggling at the corners of her mouth. "That's right. Lucy. L, U, C—"

Larry sighed. "I know how to spell it." He wrote it down. There was little else he could do. He knew what her real name was. But then, she knew what his real name was as well.

LUCY CAMPBELL

Trad

Helen was already out milking when J.J. got up. There was a pot of tea on the table. He drank a cup as he tackled the homework. By the time Helen came in again, he had battled his way through the math questions and was trying to get to grips with a history essay. Helen tiptoed around him, making fresh tea, putting out cereals and milk, slicing bread for the toaster, but he was aware of her eyes resting on the cover of his new math workbook. He thought for a moment that she might ignore it. She didn't.

"How come you're J.J. Byrne all of a sudden?"

He put down his pen a bit too hard. "Everyone in school uses their father's name. Why shouldn't I?"

"Because you're a Liddy," said Helen. "That's why."

He could hear the tension in her voice. She didn't

need to remind him of how important the name was to her, but she did it anyway. "There have always been Liddys in this house. You know that. You know it's one of the reasons Ciaran and I didn't get married. So you and Marian would have my name. You're a Liddy, J.J. Ciaran doesn't mind, so why should you?"

J.J. shrugged. "I just want Dad's name, that's all."

He knew she hadn't accepted it. She wouldn't, either. She left it, though, for the moment; put toast out on the table, spread butter on it while it was hot. There were other things she was due to find out about J.J. and his relationship with the Liddy tradition, but he was in no hurry to cause more trouble. She would find out soon enough.

Ciaran came down, closely followed by J.J.'s younger sister, Marian. They were both appallingly bright and bubbly in the mornings, unlike him and his mother, who each took at least an hour to warm to the new day. Their breezy greetings were met with moody responses.

"Anything on after school today?" said Ciaran.

"Hurling training," said J.J. "Till half six."

"I'll pick you up afterward," said Ciaran. "I'll get the beer while I'm at it."

J.J. said nothing. The beer was for the céilí that the

Liddys held on the second Saturday of every month; had held every second Saturday for generations. Helen played the concertina for the dancers and Phil Daly, a guitarist from the village, backed the tunes. For the last two years J.J. had played with them, usually on the fiddle, sometimes on the flute as well.

"We never went over those tunes," Helen was saying. "I can't believe it's Friday already. Maybe we'll get a chance this evening?"

J.J. reached for toast. He didn't need to say anything. They wouldn't go over the tunes that evening because that evening would be like every other; a mad race to pack in all the things that needed to be done.

"Is that the time?" said Ciaran.

They all turned to look at the clock. Ten minutes to eat breakfast and get to the bus. J.J. snatched a mouthful of toast and began to stuff his schoolbag.

THE CUP OF TEA

Trad

There was never enough time. The summer was always particularly busy because there was extra work to be done on the farm, but even in the winter, when the days were short and there was a more regular and manageable routine, the hours, the days, the weeks just flew by. Ciaran was a poet, born and bred in Dublin. Two of his collections had won prestigious awards. When he met Helen and came to live with her on the family farm, he had envisaged an idyllic lifestyle. His backyard was the inspirational range of limestone hills known as the Burren. He visualized himself living at ease, taking long walks, closing himself in his study for days and weeks on end and writing volume after volume of increasingly authoritative work. It had never happened. He supplemented his meager income by doing readings and workshops and school visits, but even when he managed to arrange blocks of free time for himself he never seemed to get any work done. Recently, when someone had asked him what he did for a living, he had said, "I'm a poet," and then added, "Allegedly. There's barely time to think a thought these days. And even if a thought gets thunk, there isn't time to turn it into a poem. Something is eating our time."

It depressed him, but the harder he tried to make time for his work, the faster it ran away from him.

It wasn't just the Liddys—or the Liddy–Byrnes, as some people called them—who were finding that there wasn't enough time. Everyone was having the same problem. It was understandable, perhaps, in those households where both parents were out at work all day and had to cram all their home and family life into a few short hours. But it wasn't just parents who complained of the shortage of time. Even children, it seemed, couldn't get enough of it. The old people said it was because they had too many things to do, and perhaps it was true that there were too many opportunities open to them. Apart from the ubiquitous televisions and computers there was, even in a small place like Kinvara, a plethora of after-school activities open to them, from karate to basketball to drama and back again. Even so, there ought to have been time for mooching along the country lanes, for picking blackberries, for lounging in summer meadows and watching the clouds go by, for climbing trees and making dens. There should have been time for reading books and watching raindrops run down windows, for finding patterns in the damp stains on the ceiling and for dreaming wild daydreams. There wasn't. Apart from the inevitable few who regarded it as their solemn duty, children could scarcely even find time for making mischief. Everybody in the village, in the county—in the whole country, it seemed—was chronically short of time.

"It never used to be like this," the old people said.

"It wasn't this way when we were young," said the middle-aged.

"Is this really what life's all about?" said the young, on those rare occasions when they had a moment to think about it.

For a while it was all anyone talked about, once the weather was out of the way. Then they didn't talk about it anymore. What was the point? And besides, where was the time to talk about time? People didn't call to one another's houses anymore; not to sit and chat over a cup of tea, anyway. Everyone was always on their way somewhere, or up to their eyes in something, or racing around trying to find someone, or, more often, merely trying to catch up with themselves.

J.J. only just made it to the end of the drive in time that morning. The bus arrived when it always had, traveled the same roads, made the same stops it had always made. But these days, somehow or other, it always arrived late for school. The driver went way too fast along the narrow roads, bringing himself and his passengers within an inch of their lives several times a week. It wasn't just him causing the trouble, either. Everyone drove too fast. Everyone was forever trying to make up lost time.

J.J. found an empty seat and sat down. He used to sit beside Jimmy Dowling every morning, but not anymore. Not since that day a week ago. That bad day. He hadn't been able to face the other boys since, and was learning how it felt to be one of the outsiders. He wanted to ask his mother about what they had told him, but he couldn't pluck up the courage. There must be some dark secret hidden there somewhere, or why had she never spoken about her grandfather before?

She had mentioned him, all right. He had learned quite a few of her grandfather's tunes, and he and Helen regularly played them together. But other than that she had never told him anything about the man, not even that J.J. had been named after him. In a family like theirs, that wasn't the kind of thing you kept quiet about. Not unless there was a reason.

The bus braked hard and squashed up against the hedgerow to avoid a cattle lorry coming in the other direction. Jimmy Dowling, who for some reason had been standing up, was thrown forward along the aisle between the seats. He fetched up beside the driver, who scowled at him and called back along the bus, "Stay in your seats now, you hear? No messing!"

The gears grated as he urged the old bus back up to speed, and soon they were hurtling toward Gort again. J.J. looked at his watch. They were already late. He could have sworn he saw the minute hand moving.

There were several empty seats ahead of J.J., but Jimmy Dowling passed them all by and dropped heavily into the one beside him. Was that why he'd been standing up? Was this an attempt at making up? If so, J.J. wasn't sure he was ready for it. He looked out through the muddy window.

"Are you going clubbing?" said Jimmy.

J.J. watched wet fields full of wet cattle. Was it a joke? An attempt to stir up more trouble? He glanced across at Jimmy. He was looking down at his school-bag, expressionless. In the seat behind them two girls were discussing eyeliners. It didn't appear to be a set-up. But Jimmy knew that J.J. wasn't going clubbing. The night for his age group was Saturday, and on Saturdays J.J. played for dancing. At least, he always had until now. J.J. Liddy, that was. What if J.J. Byrne wasn't into playing? What if he went clubbing instead?

"I might," he said.

Jimmy smiled. "Good man. There's a lift from the village at half nine."

The bus skidded to a halt outside the school gates. Jimmy stood up and joined the file of students getting off. "I'll meet you on the quay at twenty past. All right?"

J.J. nodded and looked at his watch again. Ten minutes late. At least they wouldn't be the only ones. All the buses were late these days.

THE RECONCILIATION
REEL

Trad

In the Garda barracks not far away, the new policeman was getting a grilling from his superior. He had contrived to put his notebook in the pocket of his trousers and his trousers through the washing machine. The trousers had come out very well. The notebook hadn't. What was sitting now on Sergeant Early's desk was little more than a lump of papier-mâché. Lucy Campbell and all the other bogus and nonbogus residents of Kinvara who had been caught after hours in Green's pub would not now be fined. Mary Green would not be fined either; nor would she be in any danger of losing her license. Garda Treacy's notebook was intact. It had not been through a washing machine or undergone any other form of abuse. But in a court of law, should it come to that, it contained only half the names. Larry O'Dwyer's sorry excuse for documentary evidence would not stand up. The case would be laughed out of court.

"Not a good start, O'Dwyer," said Sergeant Early.

Larry had to agree.

"Don't teach you about washing machines in Templemore, I suppose?"

"No, Sergeant. No, they don't." The truth was that nobody had ever taught him about washing machines. If his landlady hadn't gone out with her friends for a drink the previous evening he wouldn't have dreamed of attempting to find out about washing machines. As it was, he considered it a tremendous achievement to have made the thing work at all. But if he was looking for congratulations, he would have to look elsewhere.

"Can we rely upon you to take care of a new note-book?"

"You can, Sergeant."

"Leave it in the station when you go home every day, all right? If it looks as if it needs a wash I'll take care of it."

Garda Treacy burst out laughing, but the sergeant succeeded in keeping a straight face. Larry tried to count the raindrops on the window behind the desk.

He had to keep the lid on his temper. That was Rule Number One. If he lost it, there was no telling what havoc he might be tempted to wreak. That would do nobody any good.

"Now," said Sergeant Early, "I'll issue you with a new notebook. Go with Garda Treacy up to Des Hanlon's garage. Someone broke in there last night and stole most of his tools. Have a word with him and then take a look around." He turned to Garda Treacy. "You'll know where to start."

Treacy nodded and went out. Larry took the new notebook and trudged out behind him. People's things were important to them, he knew, especially if they needed them to make their livings. But searching for stolen things was not, Larry O'Dwyer was fairly certain, the reason that he had become a policeman.

THE DRUNKEN LANDLADY

Trad

The kitchen was full of the smell of lamb stew and fresh bread when J.J. got home. Ciaran stayed out in the yard, unloading the beer barrels into the converted barn where the dances were held. J.J. dropped his schoolbag and was putting on the kettle when Helen came in from the cheese room, which opened off the utility beside the kitchen.

"Good day?" she asked, pulling off the silly white cap that she was obliged, under EU law, to wear when she was making cheese. "Want to have a quick look at those tunes before dinner?"

J.J.'s thoughts stalled and a massive anxiety descended upon him. "I'm knackered," he said. "And I have to put on a wash."

"Do that, then," said Helen. "I'll make you a cup

of tea. It won't take long for you to get up to speed with the tunes. You know most of them anyway."

It was true. J.J. had been hearing traditional music since before he was born. He knew hundreds of tunes, possibly thousands. During the dancing class the previous week, Helen had remembered a couple of old jigs that she wanted to teach him, and they had come up with a few reels that he had known at one time but needed to go over before he could play them well enough for the dancers. Like most young people who have been brought up in the tradition, J.J. had an ability to learn new tunes that was phenomenal. He had been playing since he was five: the whistle first, then the flute, and now the fiddle as well. He had been going to workshops with top musicians around the area since he was nine or ten. He could learn those new tunes in five minutes and the others, the ones he had forgotten, would come back to him easily. All they needed to do was play them through a couple of times. But he was reluctant now to take out the instruments. If he did, he would have to tell his mother that he wouldn't be playing tomorrow, and he wasn't ready to do that. Not yet.

"Go on," Helen was saying. "Put on your wash."

J.J. ran up the stairs. Every surface in his bedroom

was littered with medals and trophies and plaques. If he jumped on the floorboards the whole room rattled. He had made, in school woodworking class, an open-fronted cabinet for displaying them all. It had brackets for mounting it on the wall, but it still sat on the floor, leaning against the chest of drawers, just another of those little jobs that were on the long finger, waiting for that imaginary time when he finally caught up with himself and had a few moments to spare.

He had amassed all the prizes over the years—for playing the fiddle and flute, for hurling, and for dancing. In his final year at primary school he had been unbeatable at step dancing. His teacher thought he could be all-Ireland champion, but secondary school put an end to her hopes for him. Michael Flatley and Riverdance might have wowed the whole country, the whole of the western world even, but they cut no ice among J.J.'s classmates in Gort. Dancing was uncool. Only nerds did it. J.J. gave it up. Playing music was a bit less unacceptable, to begin with at least, and J.J. had carried on with the fiddle and flute, attending fleadhs and piling up the medals and trophies. He would still be doing it now, if it hadn't been for the time factor.

There had been several competitions earmarked for the summer that had just passed, but somehow all the dates had come and gone without J.J., all of them lost in the headlong rush of their lives. And now there wasn't even time to wonder about it; about what it was they had been doing that was so much more important than the fleadhs.

His fiddle was hanging on the wall. It was a beautiful instrument, coveted by every fiddler who had ever played it. Its tone was vibrant and sweet, ringing through the tunes, however fast and furious their pace. For a moment J.J. allowed his eyes to rest on it, savored the little lift that the prospect of playing it always produced in his heart. He had been trained early; indoctrinated, some might even say. He was good. Playing had brought him prizes and praise. But none of these things was responsible for the soft flutter of anticipation, the itch in his fingers as they longed for the feel of the strings and the bow. J.J. played because he loved it. J.J. Liddy did, anyway. But what about J.J. Byrne?

Helen called him from the foot of the stairs.

"Coming!" he called back.

Half the clothes he owned were strewn around the floor, some dirty, some nearly clean. What did lads wear to clubs anyway? He had never been to one, nor could he remember having seen any of his friends on their way to one, or on their way back. He opened his jeans drawer. His best trousers were in there, the ones he wore to mass. They would be too smart, surely? He didn't want to look like a dork. What, then?

"J.J.?" Helen again. "Come on, we haven't much time."

He swept his way across the room, snatching up clothes with his hands, kicking them into a pile with his feet. When everything was in one heap, he bundled it up and charged down the stairs. It could all go in the wash. He would decide later what to wear.

Helen was sitting beside the range, getting the concertina out of its case. Music was always played there, in the big old kitchen. In the old days that was where the dances had been held. Helen told visitors that, and showed them the places where the flagstones had been worn down by generations of dancing feet. The conversion of the barn had been her own enterprise. Her mother, who was still living at the time, had been disgusted by the idea until she saw the result. Then even she had been forced to admit that it was a lovely place for dancing. When J.J. looked around the kitchen now, he found it hard to believe that four sets had ever had room to move in there. Four sets was thirty-two dancers; all on the go together. It was a big kitchen, but it wasn't that big. Helen, however, swore that it was true. She had played for the dancers herself, along with her mother.

As J.J. crammed the clothes into the washing machine, he heard his mother's fingers moving tentatively across the buttons of the concertina, fishing for the old tunes she wanted him to learn. He picked up three powder boxes before he found one with some left in it. Another long-finger job—tidy up the utility room. He set the program, turned on the machine, and raced up the stairs for the fiddle. But even as he lifted it from the wall he heard the knock on the door and the voice in the little porch.

"Hello?"

He should have been expecting it. It was always the way, these days. Carve out a bit of time for something and what happened? Something, or someone, came along and stole it.

ROLLING IN THE
BARREL

Trad

The visitor was Anne Korff. She didn't need to be shown the worn patches on the kitchen flags; she had come to the house many times before. Anne had been living in the area for more than twenty years, running a small publishing company producing books and maps based on the Burren. She knew the region better than many people who had lived there all their lives and was fiercely protective of anything that posed a threat to its delicate environmental balance.

J.J. came downstairs, the fiddle in one hand, the bow and rosin in the other. Anne's little terrier, Lottie, wagged her tail at him but didn't venture out from behind Anne's legs. From his bed beside the range, Bosco looked on with heroic restraint.

"Ah, you are just going to play," said Anne. "I'm disturbing you."

"Not at all," said Helen, and meant it. The hospitality of generations ran through her veins. Nothing, not even music, was more important. "We're just having a cup of tea. Sit yourself down, there."

Anne understood better than most the pressures of time. "No, really," she said. "I was just passing your door and I thought I would pop in and get a bit of cheese."

Helen sold most of her cheese to a wholesaler who distributed it to delicatessens around the country, but there were a few people, like Anne, who liked to call in and buy it direct.

"Of course," said Helen. "But you may as well have a cup of tea while you're here."

"No," said Anne. "I would love to, but I'm way behind schedule with the new book. I'm up to my eyes in editing. There just aren't enough hours in the day anymore."

"You don't have to tell me," said Helen wearily. "I'll get you some cheese, then." She moved toward the door. "A small one, is it?"

"And how's life with J.J.?" said Anne, when Helen was gone.

"Good," said J.J. automatically. "And yourself?"

"Good, good," said Anne Korff. "You're getting so

tall these days. I suppose you are going to clubs and everything now, eh?"

Her words hit J.J. in the solar plexus. Helen was already returning with the cheese, wrapped in grease-proof paper. If she had heard Anne's question, she gave no sign of it.

"That all right?" she asked.

"Perfect," said Anne. She turned to J.J. "You know your mother makes the best cheese in the country?"

"Ah, now," said Helen. She put the cheese on top of the dresser beside the door.

As Anne paid her for it, she said, "No, I was just out for a walk. Nosing around on your land. I hope you don't mind?"

"Why would I?" said Helen. "Walk where you like, Anne."

"I know that, of course," said Anne. "But I was looking at that old ring fort up at the top of your grazing land. I never knew it was there. It's not marked on any of the maps, as far as I know. Such a beautiful fort as well. So well preserved."

"I suppose it is," said Helen.

The terrier was getting bolder, venturing out from behind Anne's feet and beginning to explore the kitchen.

"No, it's just . . ." said Anne. "I see the field there has been bulldozed."

J.J. saw a hint of suspicion creep into his mother's face. The edges of the Burren contained a lot of rough, rocky land of very little use to farmers. In the past, some areas had been cleared by hand and, since the invention of bulldozers, a lot more had been mechanically cleared. It was illegal now, and had been for several years, under environmental protection legislation. J.J., like his mother, thought that Anne might be suggesting they had broken the law.

"That was a long time ago," said Helen. "When I was a child."

"Of course," said Anne. "I can see that. I was just interested to see how careful they were to preserve the fort. People in those days had such respect."

"Not just in those days," said Helen. "I don't know of any farmers who would touch a fairy ring. They'd know it would bring bad luck down upon them."

"They still believe that?" said Anne.

"Any that I know," said Helen.

The terrier was sniffing around the dresser, vacuuming up bread crumbs. J.J. could see that Bosco's patience was wearing thin.

"It's good to hear," said Anne. "But that one is such

a good one. I must put it on the map when we next revise it. Would you mind?"

"Why would I?" said Helen. She had no objection to people walking on her land, and Ciaran positively encouraged it, being of the belief that whatever the Land Registry might say, no one could really be said to own land.

"Is there a souterrain in it, do you know?" said Anne.

"No," said Helen.

"What's a souterrain?" asked J.J.

"Underground houses," said Anne. "Most of the ring forts round here have them. Some have several rooms with beautiful flagstone ceilings. Have you never been inside one?" J.J. shook his head. He hadn't, though he knew now what she was talking about. A lot of his friends had been inside places like that. They called them caves.

"I will show you," said Anne Korff. "Come down to my house one fine day. There is one fairly near where I live. I will show you." She turned back to Helen. "So, this ring fort. Has it ever been excavated?"

Helen didn't get as far as answering. J.J. could have prevented what happened next; he had seen it coming a long way off. The talk of the souterrain had distracted him, and while he wasn't looking, Lottie had discovered Bosco's food bowl. There was nothing in it, but that didn't prevent the old dog from being fiercely possessive about it. There was an explosion of barks and yelps. Suddenly there seemed to be dogs everywhere. Everyone started yelling at them at once, and at the first safe opportunity Anne whipped the quivering terrier up under her arm, from where it peered out at everyone with a victimized expression.

"Sorry about that," said Anne. "We'll get out of your way now."

"Do you need a lift?" said Helen.

"No, no. My car is at the bottom of the hill."

And she was gone.

Helen sat down and picked up the concertina. J.J. began to rosin his bow. But before they could start playing, Ciaran came in.

"What did Anne Korff want?" he asked but didn't wait for an answer. "That stew must be ready now. Where's Marian?"

"Learning her lines for the play," said Helen. "But no one's eating anything until we've gone over these tunes."

Ciaran went off to find Marian, and Helen started fingering the keys again. She gave J.J. an A and he tuned the fiddle. Then she began fishing again, and before long a haunting little jig began to emerge from the bellows. J.J. had never heard it before.

"It's lovely," he said, when she had played it through twice. "What's it called?"

"I don't remember the name of it. My grandfather used to play it."

Helen's grandfather. His great-grandfather. J.J. went cold again. "On the flute, was it?" he asked.

Helen looked up. "How did you know that?"

He didn't answer.

"J.J.?" Helen could see from his expression that something was wrong. "Has someone been telling you stories?"

Ciaran and Marian breezed in. "You're overruled," said Ciaran. "Two against two. Maz has to get to drama. We have to eat now."

This time, neither J.J. nor Helen had any resistance to offer.

THE CONCERTINA
REEL

Trad

"Right," said Ciaran, plonking the stewpot down on the table and sitting down behind it. "Before our mouths are full, and before the phone rings, and before the goats break out again—"

"And before Anne Korff comes back for her cheese," J.J. broke in.

"What?" said Helen.

"And before we start talking about Anne Korff's cheese," Ciaran went on determinedly, "I have something to say."

"You'd better be quick then," said Marian, ladling stew onto her plate.

"I will," said Ciaran. "What do you want for your birthday?"

Marian passed the ladle to Helen, who dipped it

into the stew before she realized who Ciaran was talk-ing to. "You don't mean me?"

"I do," said Ciaran.

"It can't be my birthday again already," said Helen. "I've only just had one."

"I know how you feel," said Ciaran. "It seems as if your last birthday was only a month ago, but that short month was in fact a short year. In three weeks' time, which will feel to us all like three days, you will be having another one."

"Oh, no," said Helen. "Forty-five!"

"Forty-six, actually," said Marian, who was always right.

"I can't be!" said Helen.

"Twenty-one, then," said Ciaran. "We don't mind. But what do you want?"

Helen sat back and dropped the ladle. J.J. took it and filled her plate, then his own.

"I don't know," said Helen. "There isn't really anything I want."

"Good," said Ciaran. "That's easy then."

"Time," said Helen. "That's what I want. Time."

"I see," said Ciaran thoughtfully. "And how would madam like her time served? A week in the Algarve perhaps? Two weeks in Spiddal?"

Helen shook her head. "Not that kind of time. Ordinary, run-of-the-mill time. A few more hours in every day."

"Tall order," said Marian.

"Not possible," said J.J.

"Never say never," said Ciaran. "Where there's a will there's a what?"

"A big family argument, usually," said Marian.

"There's always a way," said Ciaran. "Anything can be done. So that'll be J.J.'s present. What do you want from the rest of us?"

But Helen wasn't in the mood. Her mind was on what J.J. had said earlier, about her grandfather. It was time for him to learn a bit of family history.

Ciaran and Helen went out to get the goats in, leaving J.J. and Marian to clear the kitchen and wash up. J.J. waited until the worst of the clattering was over, then said, as casually as he could, "What are the fellas wearing to the clubs these days?"

His sister saw straight through him. "Clubs? Are you going clubbing?"

"No! I was just wondering, that's all."

"Are you going tomorrow? Have you got a girlfriend?"

"Of course I haven't got a girlfriend!"

"But you're going clubbing? Are you? Seriously? Does Mum know?"

There was no point in trying to pull the wool over Marian's eyes. Nothing escaped her. Besides, it was suddenly a great relief to have a confidante.

"Not yet," said J.J. "Don't tell her, will you? I might not go at all."

"You have to tell her. You can't just dump her in it for the dance."

"Why not? She doesn't need me. Herself and Phil did it for years on their own."

"It's different now. You're part of the band. Half the tunes they play are your tunes."

"She doesn't need me, Maz. Anyway, if you're so worried about it, why don't you play?"

"Because I'm not good enough, that's why."

"You are. You're every bit as good as I was when I started doing it."

It was true. He and Helen were always trying to persuade her to join in. She already had nearly as many medals and trophies as J.J., and she was still in primary school. She was still dancing and she would, J.J. knew, carry on when she went to secondary. Marian would never be influenced by what other people thought of her.

"So?" he said. "What do fellas wear to go clubbing?"

Marian shrugged. "I don't know. And if I did I wouldn't tell you."

J.J. had no chance to press her. Ciaran was at the front door, bellowing. Marian looked at the clock, grabbed her script, and raced out.

J.J. finished the washing-up on his own. His fiddle was on the settle where he had left it. He resisted the temptation to pick it up, and when he had finished cleaning up the kitchen he put his wet clothes in the dryer and went upstairs to have another think about what to wear.

His new sneakers would do, anyway. They weren't a fashionable brand—Ciaran wouldn't allow anything made by sweatshop labor into the house—but they were cool enough. That was one decision made, but J.J. found he couldn't get any further. He had no sense of fashion at all. Helen still bought all his clothes. Should he ring Jimmy and ask him? Would he sound like a fool? Probably. But it would be better than looking like one. He went downstairs to the phone, but he was cut off at the pass by Helen, coming back in from the milking.

"Are you busy?" she asked him.

Those words invariably preceded a request for help with something. J.J. searched for an excuse, but he was too slow. He was wrong, this time, as well.

"I wanted to have a word with you," Helen said. "About my grandfather."

THE WISE MAID

Trad

The new policeman was off duty, driving along the narrow roads that ran through the heart of the Burren. He was driving very slowly, partly because he hadn't been driving very long and wasn't at all comfortable with the idea, and partly because he was looking for something. What it was that he was looking for was unclear to him, but he assumed, or at least he hoped, that if he saw it he would recognize it.

He pulled off the road to allow another car to go by. It didn't need the whole width of the road, but Larry felt it was probably safer to let it have it anyway. Then, since he had found a convenient place to leave the car for a while, he decided to get out and take a stroll around. He climbed the nearest wall and wandered across the rocks, stepping from one slab to the next, avoiding the treacherous cracks between them. As he walked he wondered if it would be appropriate to pay a visit to Green's that evening. When he thought about Sergeant Early and Garda Treacy he was fairly sure what their reaction would be. But he was off duty. There was nothing in the rule book, as far as he could remember, that made the local pubs off limits to him.

He turned to his left and climbed a rocky hillock. When he got to the top, a spectacular view revealed itself: gray hill after gray hill stretching away until they met the hazy horizon. Westward the sun, huge and yellow, was sinking fast. The sight reminded him of home and that elusive thing he had come here in order to find. It was like looking for a needle in a haystack. No. Needles in haystacks didn't come close to describing the magnitude of the task he had in hand.

And time was slipping away much, much too fast.

THE STONY STEPS

Trad

J.J. was curious about what Helen had to say, but at the same time he dreaded it.

"Let's have a cup of tea," said Helen.

Tea was their fuel and their comfort, snatched wherever possible during their frantic days. When the range was lit in the winter, the kettle was always sitting on it, ready for when it would next be needed. That day hadn't been cold enough for the range, but the sitting room was always inclined to be damp, so while Helen boiled the electric kettle and made the tea, J.J. lit a few briquettes in the fireplace. Then, without telling Helen, he took the phone off the hook. Marian was staying overnight with a friend when her drama group was over, and Ciaran was going straight on to Galway after dropping her, to a meeting of the local antiwar group. Provided no one dropped by the house, J.J. and his mother might get a rare chance to talk in peace.

The light was almost gone from the day. While the tea brewed in front of the fledgling flames, J.J. drew the curtains and Helen rummaged in the cupboard against the wall beside the piano. She returned with a large, tatty brown envelope, and while J.J. poured the tea, she examined its contents. When he handed her a cup, she gave him a dog-eared black-and-white photograph, then pulled her chair around beside his so that they could look at it together.

The frame of the picture was filled by the front of the house, the Liddy house where they were sitting now. In those days it would have been fairly new and, in comparison to the average Irish farmhouse, fairly grand. The Liddys then, if not now, were influential people. In front of the house, seven people were standing: three men, a woman, and three children—a girl and two boys. All of them held musical instruments. All of them wore serious, even stern expressions. From what J.J. had seen of old photographs, that was not unusual.

"It was taken in 1935," said Helen. "The woman with the fiddle was my grandmother, your great-grandmother. This fellow here, beside her, is Gilbert Clancy."

"Gilbert Clancy? Let's see." J.J. had heard about Gilbert Clancy before. He had known the legendary blind piper, Garrett Barry, and had passed on a large part of his repertoire to his better-known son, Willie Clancy.

"Gilbert was a great friend of the Liddys," said Helen. "He was often in this house."

"Was Willie ever here?"

"Plenty of times," said Helen. She pointed to another of the men in the photograph. "That's your great-grandfather. He made that flute himself, out of the spoke of a cartwheel."

"Are you serious?"

"God's truth," said Helen.

J.J. held the photograph closer to the light and examined the instrument. The focus was sharp, but the figures were too far from the lens for the details to be clear. He could see, though, that the flute was very plain, with no decoration of any kind. If it had joints, they were invisible.

"He wasn't known as an instrument maker," Helen went on, "but he made a few flutes and whistles in his time. Micho Russell told me once that he had played a whistle my grandfather made and he had liked it enough to try to buy it. But of all the instruments he made, that flute there was the best. He loved it. Could hardly stop playing it. Wherever he went, that flute went with him. They say that he was so afraid of losing it that he engraved his name on it, up at the top."

"What happened to it?" asked J.J. "Where is it now?"

"That's the story I want to tell you, J.J. It's a sad story, but when you hear it you might understand why music has always been so important to me. The music and the Liddy name."

Helen topped up their mugs and leaned back in her chair. "There were always dances in this house, going way back. As long as there was music, the Liddys have been musicians. You'd think it was simple, wouldn't you, looking at it now? A harmless pastime? Better than harmless, even. Healthy. But in those days dance music had its enemies."

"What kind of enemies?" asked J.J.

"Powerful ones," said Helen. "The clergy."

"What—the priests?"

"The priests, yes. And above them the bishops, and above them the cardinals."

"But why?"

"It's not an easy question. There's an obvious answer, which is that young people gathered together from all over the parish—beyond it, even. The dances were great social occasions. Men and women mixed together and got to know each other. Pretty much like the clubs and discos now, I suppose. Everyone would have a few drinks and let their hair down a bit. The clergy maintained that the dances led to immoral behavior."

"People still say that," said J.J., "about discos and clubs." He spotted a window of opportunity opening. Would now be a good moment to tell her?

"They do," said Helen. "And I suppose they're right, according to their own frames of reference. Things go on in those places that every parent would have reason to worry about."

J.J.'s window slammed shut. Helen reached out and dropped another briquette onto the fire, sending up a little plume of sparks.

"But there was another, less obvious reason that the priests, or some of them at least, hated our music. The Irish—the majority of us anyway—have been Catholic for hundreds of years. If you look at it simplistically, you could say that the priests wielded total control over our lives and our beliefs. But the truth wasn't so simple."

"It never is," said J.J.

"It never is," Helen repeated. "There were older,

more primitive beliefs in Ireland that went back even further than the Church. They went back thousands, not hundreds of years. In some small ways they're still with us today."

"Like what?" said J.J.

"The fairy folk," said Helen, "and all the stories and superstitions that surround them."

"But that's not still with us," said J.J. "Nobody believes in any of that these days."

Helen shrugged. "Maybe not. But remember what Anne Korff was talking about today? The forts? How the farmers won't clear them from the land?"

"They're historical monuments, aren't they?"

"Perhaps that's all it is now," said Helen. "But I'm not sure. That one in our top meadow isn't recorded anywhere. It doesn't have any kind of preservation order on it. So will you bulldoze it when you take over the farm?"

J.J. thought about it and found that he wouldn't. Deep down, in a place in himself that he had never visited, he found that he was as superstitious about the fort as his mother was; as her mother and her grandparents would have been. He shook his head.

"No," said Helen. "And you don't even believe in fairies. My mother did, you know. And in my grandparents' time everyone did. People still saw them, or believed that they did. And loads of people claimed to have heard their music."

"But that's crazy stuff," said J.J.

"Maybe," said Helen. "Maybe not. In any event, the priests were of your opinion. It was more than crazy, according to them. It was dangerous and subversive. But they couldn't knock those old beliefs out of people, no matter how hard they tried or what hellfire they threatened them with. The fairies and the country people just went too far back together. And the one thing that everyone agreed upon, whether they had heard it themselves or not, was that our music— our jigs and our reels and our hornpipes and our slow airs—was given to us by the fairies."

A cold little shiver trickled down J.J.'s spine. It wasn't the first time he had heard the old association, but it was the first time it had touched him.

"So," Helen went on, "the priests could do nothing to stamp out the fairy beliefs. They had tried and failed for long enough. But there was one thing they might be able to get rid of, and that was the music. If they succeeded in that, there was a chance that the rest of the superstitions would follow of their own accord.

"They weren't all like that. There were some priests

who were very tolerant of the old traditions. There were even some who played a few tunes themselves. But there were others who broke up musical gatherings and dances wherever they found them and did their utmost to stamp out the music. Then, in 1935, the year this photo was taken, they added a new, powerful weapon to their armory. It was called the Public Dance Hall Act."

J.J. was losing interest. He got more than enough history at school. "What's this got to do with your granddad?" he said.

"I'm getting there," said Helen. "Basically, until then most of the dances had been like our céilís. They were held in people's houses or sometimes, in summer, at a crossroads. People paid to get into them, to cover the cost of the drink and the musicians. There might even have been a bit of profit in it for the house owner, though that was never why we had dances here. But the new act, which was passed by the government under pressure from the Church, made the house dances illegal. From that time onward, all dances had to be held in the parish hall, where the priest could keep an eye on the goings-on. It nearly worked, too, because it wasn't long before other kinds of music began to get popular. We very nearly lost our musical tradition."

"But people could still play, couldn't they? In the pub or in their houses?"

"They could, but sessions are a relatively new thing, you know—people playing tunes while other people sit around and talk. I don't like it myself. This music is dance music, J.J. It always was. That's why I made sure you and Maz learned to dance. Even if you never do it again, you understand the music from the inside out."

J.J. nodded. He had been to a lot of fleadhs and heard a lot of people playing. You could almost always tell from their playing whether they knew how to dance or not.

"Anyway," Helen went on, "the long and the short of it was that the house dances were in danger of dying out. You could hold a dance if you didn't charge an entrance fee, but there weren't many people around in those days who could afford to do that."

"But the Liddys could," said J.J.

"Yup. The Liddys could. We weren't rich by modern standards, but we were pretty well off by the standards of those days. And we had one big advantage over a lot of the other houses that used to hold dances. We didn't have to pay the musicians. We were the musicians."

GARRETT BARRY'S JIG

Trad

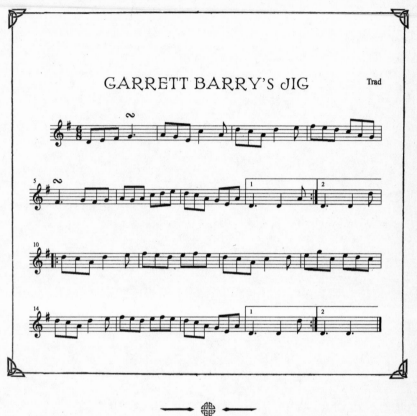

The new policeman went into Kinvara, got a bite to eat in Rosaleen's, and made his way down the street to Green's. He was on the early side, he knew. Sessions never got going much before ten o'clock. He had thought long and hard about whether it would be better to arrive early or late and had eventually decided on early. If he arrived when the session had already started, there was a danger that the shock of being joined by a policeman would knock the spirit out of the music. Getting there early would give Mary Green a chance to get used to the idea, and with luck, he would be able to convince the musicians that he wasn't there in any official capacity.

At the door he paused, his fiddle in his hand. Perhaps it wasn't such a good idea after all? His presence was sure to inhibit the others, and Mary Green would probably hunt them all out into the street at twelve o'clock on the dot. He would ruin it for everyone. Maybe it would be better if he just went home and had a tune there with the others, free from the tyranny of the licensing laws?

No. He'd better stay. He'd set out to investigate something, after all. There might be clues anywhere. You could never know what you might hear.

He met with a frosty reception in Green's. Mary was a generous woman, but it was beyond even her powers of hospitality to make a man welcome when, just the previous night, he had raided her premises. Some of the same customers were in that evening, and it didn't take them long to reveal Larry's identity to the ones who didn't yet know it. One of the musicians turned round the moment he set eyes on the policeman and went up the road to play in Winkles instead. The others stood around the bar and engaged in a game of musical politics that might have gone on all night if it hadn't been for a piper who lived locally. He didn't drink and he couldn't abide standing around. He was there for the music, not for the politics, and he was always gone before closing time anyway.

"I suppose we'll play a tune," he said to Larry.

"I suppose we will," said Larry.

By the end of the first set of tunes there wasn't a musician left standing. Whatever his profession, Larry's fiddle playing left little to be desired. No one in the room had ever heard anything quite like it. Within minutes everyone had tuned up their instruments and the music was off again.

Mary Green brought more drinks. Larry felt the music race in his blood, linking his past to his present, bringing him home. For the first time since he had arrived in Kinvara, the new policeman was happy.

THE TEETOTALLER

Trad

"This parish was unlucky," said Helen. "Father Doherty was a good priest in a lot of ways, so I've been told, but he was one of the worst where the music was concerned. A Sunday hardly passed without him ranting from the pulpit about the terrible vengeance God would wreak on those who believed in fairies and danced to their evil tunes. Even before the act was passed, he walked the roads at night, barging into any house where he heard music and browbeating everyone he found there. He broke a man's fiddle once, under his boot. But out of all his parishioners, there was none that made him as angry as my grandfather.

"The hatred was mutual. J.J.—" Helen paused. "Did I tell you he was called J.J.? That you were named after him?"

"You didn't," said J.J. "But someone else did."

"Who?"

"Never mind. Go on."

Helen hesitated, wondering whether to press him, then decided against it. "He used to bar the door against Father Doherty and play away while he battered on the door and yelled. Then, on Sundays, he used to turn up in the church and sit through all the tirades as if they didn't concern him in the slightest. Father Doherty couldn't take it. He was used to being obeyed. The act was barely made law when he turned the Liddys in for holding a house dance. They weren't the only ones either. There were a good few prosecutions that year, and a lot of them were successful. People got stuck with fines they could never afford to pay. The act was working. But it didn't work against the Liddys. People told my grandfather later that Father Doherty had threatened them with eternal damnation if they didn't stand up in court and swear that they'd been charged an entrance fee at the door of the dance. But for all their fear of the priest and the power vested in him, there wasn't one person who would betray the Liddys. That's how highly the family was regarded in the parish back then."

Helen stopped for a moment, and J.J. saw a look of

fierce pride in her eyes. Then it collapsed and she turned her gaze to the flames. "But that was before."

J.J. waited. Helen took a deep breath. "The case was thrown out. My grandparents held a dance to celebrate. It was high summer and the nights were long and warm. The dancers spilled out of the house into the yard, and after a while the musicians followed them out there. Everyone said the craic was mighty. There had never been a dance to equal it. Until Father Doherty turned up.

"He was so furious that not even my grandfather could keep on playing. He was red in the face and shaking with rage.

"'You think you got the better of me, don't you?' he said.

"Father Doherty was not a young man. My grand-mother was concerned for him. Despite all that had happened, she didn't want him to have a seizure, on her doorstep or anywhere else. She invited him to step inside the house and have a cup of tea.

"'I'll never again set foot in that iniquitous house,' he said to her. 'And I'll tell you another thing as well. I will put an end to this devil's music.'

"He snatched the flute out of my grandfather's hand and marched out of the yard. My grandfather ran after him, but he was—you have to believe this, J.J.—he was a gentle man. He loved that flute above all else that he owned, but he would not resort to violence to get it back. Father Doherty walked away from this house with the flute that night, seventy years ago, and that was the last time that anyone ever saw him."

"What?" said J.J.

"He disappeared. He was never seen again."

"But . . . you mean they never even found a body?"

Helen shook her head. "Nothing. To this day no one knows what happened to him. But unfortunately, people being what they are, a nasty rumor began to go around."

"That your grandfather killed him?"

Helen nodded.

"And did he?" said J.J.

"Of course he didn't."

"How do you know?"

"I just know, J.J. He didn't have it in him. He hated authority, but he wasn't a murderer."

"What happened to the flute?"

"Gone, too. It was never seen again."

"That's weird," said J.J. "How could someone just disappear?"

"I don't know any more than you do," said Helen.

"It happens sometimes, though. People do disappear. They searched high and low for him, but they never found any trace."

J.J. turned back to the photograph with renewed interest. His great-grandfather was a big man, but J.J. could see nothing in his face that suggested he was capable of such a violent crime.

"The parish was divided," Helen went on. "A lot of people turned against the Liddys, but a lot more stayed loyal to us. Even so, for a long time after that midsummer's night there wasn't a note played in this house. It was more than a month later that Gilbert Clancy turned up in the yard. He had been far away when Father Doherty went missing and had only just heard about it. He listened while my grandfather told him the whole story. When he was finished, Gilbert said, 'Well. That priest has succeeded in his aim, hasn't he?'

"My grandfather asked him what he meant. When I was a child he told me the story many times, and what Gilbert said to him. 'Your man has brought silence into one of the greatest houses for music that there ever was. He has taken more than your flute from you, J.J.'

"My grandfather sat and thought about that for a

long, long time. Then he got up and went out to the back room that he used to use for his workshop. By the time he came back, Gilbert Clancy was already warming up his flute and my grandmother's fiddle had been taken down from the wall and dusted off.

"And from that day to this, J.J., there has always been music in this house."

THE PRIEST AND HIS
BOOTS

Trad

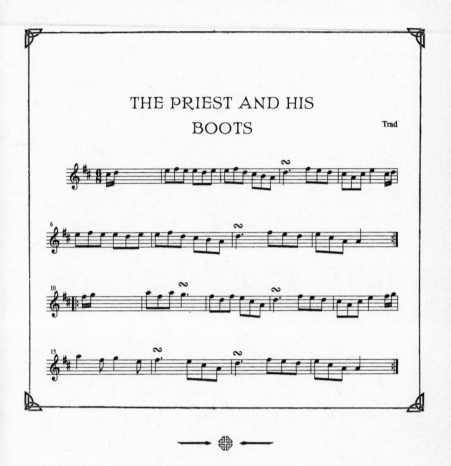

There was only one hairy patch in the whole glorious evening of tunes. They'd been playing for about half an hour when an old man came into the pub and sat on a high stool at the bar. He was vaguely familiar to Larry, but age did strange things to people's faces and besides, since Larry could barely remember his own name at times, he was unlikely to remember anyone else's.

The piper launched into a set of hornpipes and Larry forgot everything except the music, but when he next looked up the old man was still there, and was staring straight at him. After the next set of tunes, he got down from the stool and tacked across the pub to where the musicians were sitting. He declined the low stool that was offered to him by one of the nearest listeners. Nothing would do him but to push his way through and squeeze into the corner of the padded bench beside Larry O'Dwyer.

"How're you doing?" he said.

"Great," said Larry. "And yourself?"

"Very good as well," said the old man. He pulled a well-worn tin whistle out of his pocket and waited politely until someone started a tune, then joined in. More tunes followed, and the old man said nothing else to Larry, or to anyone else either, until the piper's early departure caused a mild distraction among the company. Then, while everyone else's attention was elsewhere, he leaned in close to Larry and said, "What name are you going by this weather?"

After a few panic-stricken moments Larry remembered. "O'Dwyer," he said, in an unnecessarily conspiratorial whisper. "Larry O'Dwyer."

The old man extended a large paw and grasped Larry's hand. "Patrick O'Hare," he said. "Even after all these years. Still Patrick O'Hare."

"Of course you are," said Larry, still failing to remember the man. "And why wouldn't you be?"

But Patrick O'Hare had already retrieved his hand and was starting off a lovely old reel on the whistle. One by one, the other musicians joined in.

✪ ✪ ✪

J.J. Byrne had not enjoyed a very long existence. J.J. was all Liddy again, after what his mother had told him, and he was bursting to play tunes and fill the old house with music again.

"You're not to move, now, you hear me?" he said. "I don't care what needs doing. This is the first installment of your birthday present."

She followed his instructions and stayed where she was while he made more tea and brought in the instruments. He brought in his flute as well, even though he rarely played it these days. It made him feel closer to his maligned namesake.

J.J. learned his great-grandfather's jig on it, and the other tune that Helen wanted to teach him, then he changed to the fiddle while they ran through some of the tunes they wanted to play the following evening. There was no more question in J.J.'s mind of going clubbing. One day, perhaps, but not tomorrow.

Time flew by as usual, but they carried on playing, just for the pleasure of being together and giving some of their favorite tunes an airing. When they finally wound down, too tired to play anymore, J.J. picked up the photo again.

"Who are the children?"

Helen looked over his shoulder. "That's my mother, with the concertina, and her two brothers. They both died young, which is how she came to inherit the farm. She was the only one who survived. They were hard times."

There were more photographs lying facedown on top of their shabby envelope. Helen reached out to stop him, but J.J.'s hand got there first. He checked with her eyes, saw acceptance in them, understood that he had not yet learned the last of the Liddy secrets. He turned the photos over, not at all sure that he was ready for any more surprises. But the first one was innocent enough. A woman, standing at the head of a gray donkey. In the cart behind it was a bare-footed child, a girl.

"My mother and my grandmother," said Helen.

The next photo was more formal: a studio shot of a young couple, he standing with his cap in his hands, she sitting in a straight-backed chair. Both of them stared stiffly into the camera lens.

"My grandparents again," said Helen. "J.J. and Helen."

J.J. grinned at the correspondence and turned over the final photograph. It had been taken in a hay meadow in midsummer. On the left was a neat, new haycock. Others were spread across the field behind it. To the right of the frame were two musicians: a young woman with a concertina, sitting on the tail of an empty hay wagon, and, standing behind her, a young man holding a fiddle. The woman's hair was dark and wild; most of it had escaped from its ponytail. Her face was either flushed or sunburned, and wore a bright smile. But the fiddler's face was turned away from the camera, revealing nothing other than the graceful curve of his brow and cheekbone beneath a mop of sandy hair.

"My mother," said Helen. "She was a great player."

"And who's the man?"

Helen hesitated. In the silence the reddened briquettes collapsed in on themselves and began to blaze again.

"My father," Helen said at last, and J.J. realized he had already guessed it. He leaned back in the chair, the photo in one hand, his fiddle in the other.

"That was the only photograph that was ever taken of him," Helen went on. "My mother never spoke about him. At least, not until she was dying and then . . . well . . . she used to ramble. Her mind, you know . . ." She tore herself away from memories that were clearly disturbing. "Anyway, I was pregnant with you before she gave me that photo. She was still madly in love with him, even then."

"Who was he?" said J.J.

His mother smiled and shrugged. "Bit of a wild man from what I can make out. A wandering musician. For a year or two he used to come and go. Lad, they called him. If he had another name my mother never heard it. Just Lad. A great fiddler, though. The best my grandparents ever heard. And handsome enough to charm the birds out of the trees."

She took the photo from J.J. and gazed at it wistfully. "I wish he hadn't turned away just at that moment," she said. "I dream about him, you know. I'd give anything to know what he looked like."

"What happened to him?"

Helen shrugged. "He came and went for a while. He and my mother started courting; became lovers, eventually. Then one day he went away and he didn't come back."

"Another disappearing act," said J.J.

"Yes. Not such an unusual one, though. When the priest—a different one, obviously—found out that my mother was pregnant, he tried to persuade my parents to send her away and have the baby put up for adoption. Single mothers weren't acceptable in those days."

J.J. nodded. The Magdalene Laundries had been all over the news recently. A lot of innocent girls had been locked up to keep them hidden away from society.

"My grandparents wouldn't hear of it, thank God," said Helen. "So there was another reason for the Liddys to be scorned by some of the locals. An unmarried mother in the family."

"Two in a row now," said J.J.

Helen laughed. "The thing was," she said, "they were all convinced that Lad would come back. The last time he went away, he left something behind at the house. It was the only thing he owned, and they couldn't believe he wouldn't come back for it."

"What was it?" said J.J.

"His fiddle," said Helen. "You have it there in your hand."

THE FAIR-HAIRED BOY

Trad

Mary Green had never, to her knowledge, been in the position of having to throw a policeman out of her pub. She felt obliged to do it all the same. Larry didn't look as though he was about to jump up and arrest everyone, but you could never be sure.

She waited for a break in the music. "I'm going to have to ask you to finish up now," she said.

Phil Daly stopped tuning his guitar and looked up. "You're joking," he said. "It can't be that time already?"

Everyone turned to look at the clock behind the bar. It was a new one, with hands that were designed so that the observer thought they were suffering from double vision. It meant that it took awhile for everyone to figure out what it was actually reading.

"I don't know what happens to the time these days," said Laura, the flute player.

"It's mad," said Jim, letting the air out of his melodeon's bellows and fixing the strap.

"It's mad, all right," said Larry. "It never used to be like this."

"True for you," said Patrick O'Hare.

"What started it all?" said Larry. "When did time start disappearing so fast?"

"It's just because we're getting older," said Laura.

"It isn't," said Phil. "Even the kids are running round like headless chickens these days."

"'Twas the EU started it," said Patrick. "There was all the time in the world before we joined Europe and started getting all the subsidies."

"What have subsidies got to do with it?" said Laura.

"All the time-saving devices we bought with the new money," said Patrick. "Big fast tractors and bale wrappers and washing machines. And do we have more time on account of them all?"

"I think it was the Celtic Tiger," said Jim. "We sold our souls to the stock market."

Larry plucked his strings and adjusted his tuning. The conversation, as far as he could see, was going nowhere. "One for the road," he said.

Mary Green was hovering. "Please, lads," she said. "Come on now."

"They'll hardly arrest him," said Jim, unfastening his bellows again.

"They might," said Laura.

Larry was already starting a tune. "Let 'em try," he said, and unleashed the power of his bowing arm.

J.J. lay in bed. He had a hurling match the following day, and he had to be up early to get a few things done before it. He needed all the sleep he could get, but it wouldn't come to him.

How was it that in his fifteen years of life his mother had never spoken to him about her father? Even more amazing was that he had never thought to ask her; never even been curious. Did it happen in other families as well? Did all parents construct a mental map for their children, with huge areas of their lives outside its borders? Did every family have hidden territories, so cleverly concealed that they became completely invisible?

As if disappearing fathers and priests weren't enough, J.J. was worried about his friendship with Jimmy as well. They had been pals since primary school. He had forgiven Jimmy for what he had said about his great-grandfather. Sometime in the future he might even talk to him about it; tell him the Liddy side of the story. But in the meantime there was the problem of the club. Jimmy had swallowed his pride to invite him. It was a peace offering, and if J.J. rejected it by not turning up, there might never be another chance to mend the friendship.

He turned over in bed. A heavy, windblown shower galloped across the roof, paused, then galloped back again. He'd have to come up with an excuse for Jimmy. Maybe he could pretend to be ill? No. It wouldn't work. Too many people would see him playing at the céilí. What if he just said his parents wouldn't allow him to go? Blame them? Complain about them?

He couldn't do it. Another time, perhaps, but not just now. He couldn't betray the trust his mother had placed in him that evening. He could see her face now, the vulnerability in it as she talked about her father. She had never, ever seen him. There was a hole in her life where he ought to have been.

J.J. would make it up to her. He would be there beside her tomorrow, playing for the house dance; honoring all the Liddys that had gone before him. He was determined to do something else for her as well. He would get her what she wanted for her birthday.

He didn't know how he would do it, but one way or another he was going to buy her some time.

It was three o'clock in the morning when the new policeman finally rolled out of the pub. His memory was never his strongest feature, but he had an uneasy feeling that at some point during the last three hours he had threatened Mary Green with arrest if she didn't bring the musicians another drink. And then another.

He had danced as well. Patrick O'Hare had been responsible for that, announcing it to the whole room and calling for a clear space without even warning him first. Sergeant Early would not be impressed. With luck, the event would not come to his notice. There was nothing he could do about it now, anyway.

A light drizzle was falling as he walked up the street. He hoped it wouldn't penetrate the fiddle case, because there was no question of getting back into the car. He wasn't drunk, exactly, but even without any drink in him at all he wasn't certain that he could be considered fit to drive. The car could stay where it was. He was off duty for the next two days and had no plans for going anywhere. And as for getting home, he didn't need it for that, either.

TOMORROW MORNING

Trad

It poured rain all morning. The goats stood in their shelter, looking gloomy and steadfastly refusing to go near the "haylage" they were offered.

"They can do without," said Ciaran. "They'll eat it if they get hungry enough."

"They might," said Helen. "And we might wind up having to buy more hay."

J.J. fed the kids. They were getting big and rebellious now, standing on their hind legs to look over the bottom door of their shed and shoving J.J. around when he came in with their buckets of milk. It was high time to wean them and turn them out with the rest of the herd.

When he'd finished, J.J. took a shower and laid his books out on the kitchen table. There was a history essay that should have been finished by the beginning of the summer holidays, more than three months ago now, and the teacher was getting apoplectic about it. He made a bit of progress between the comings and goings of the household, and Marian even sat for a while and helped him when she came in from her slumber party.

At midday his hurling coach rang. Marian was in the sitting room working on her script again and J.J. heard her pick up the extension, then put it down again. The coach told him that the match had been abandoned because of a waterlogged pitch. J.J. breathed a huge sigh of relief and returned to his books. A minute later the phone rang again.

"I'm not here," said Helen, charging in with an armload of eggs. "I have to finish those cheeses off before they go blue on me."

J.J. answered it. It was Jimmy.

"How's it going, J.J.?"

J.J. heard the background noise of the phone line alter as someone picked up the extension, but he was too flustered to notice whether they hung up or not.

"Good," he said. "The match was rained off."

"Sound," said Jimmy. "You coming tonight, so?"

J.J. was wrong footed. He had eventually gone to sleep without deciding what he was going to say. With

Helen standing at the sink behind him, washing the eggs, he couldn't come out with a pack of lies. But if he said no, Jimmy might never speak to him again. He needed time but, as always, he didn't have it.

"I suppose so," was the best he could come up with. It didn't sound convincing, but Jimmy heard what he wanted to hear.

"Good stuff," he said. "You know what I was thinking? The bus doesn't get back here until about two o'clock in the morning."

"Oh," said J.J. Maybe this was his way of getting off the hook? But Jimmy had a solution.

"You could stay at my place if you wanted to save dragging your parents out."

J.J.'s heart sank. Jimmy was bending over backward to make up with him.

"Fair dues to you, Jimmy," he said. "It's a great idea."

"See you, then," said Jimmy. "Twenty past nine on the quay."

J.J. put the phone down and stared at it.

"What's a great idea?" said Helen.

"Nothing," said J.J. He went into the sitting room, where Marian was lounging beside the fire, marking up her script with a red pen.

"Were you listening in on my phone call?"

"What phone call?"

"Were you?"

"Sod off, J.J. I'm busy."

He went out, slamming the door behind him. What did it matter, anyway?

J.J. had to clear away the essay for lunch and before he had time to set it out again Phil and his girlfriend, Carol, arrived to help get the barn ready for the céilí.

J.J. went out with them, and Helen and Ciaran joined them a few minutes later. Carol worked in a pub in Ballyvaughan and got all the soft drinks and crisps at wholesale prices. There was no charge to get into the céilí, on an old point of Liddy principle, but the dance classes on the other Saturdays made more than was needed to cover the cost of drinks and snacks.

The rain had stopped and the sky was clear again. It wasn't cold, but Ciaran lit the stove anyway. The barn was an old building, and even in the best of weather it always needed a bit of help to dry out.

"Have you met our new policeman?" said Phil.

"No," said Helen.

"I didn't know we had one," said J.J.

"Some character," said Phil.

"Haven't you seen him?" said Carol to Helen. "He's gorgeous."

"Is he?" said Phil gloomily. "I was afraid he might be."

"He certainly is," said Carol. "He should be in the movies, that one."

"Some fiddle player, too," said Phil.

"He plays the fiddle?" said Helen.

"That's all we need in Kinvara," said Ciaran. "Another fiddle player. You can't spit round here without hitting one."

"Ah, you should hear him, though," said Phil. "He was in Green's last night. Beautiful, beautiful music."

"In Green's? A guard?"

"And he dances," said Carol. She was a dancer herself, and a good one; one of the regulars at the Liddy céilís. "You should see him, Helen. Light as a feather."

"You're having us on," said Ciaran.

"No, I swear it," said Phil. "It's true. He busted us on Thursday and played with us all night on Friday."

Helen laughed. "Sounds like my kind of guard. Better get him up here."

"I never thought of that," said Phil. "I should have asked him. I wonder, would he come?"

"Do you know where he lives?" said J.J.

"No," said Phil. "I could ask around, though. Someone's sure to know."

They went off; two people with a mission. Ciaran went back to his study, Helen to the cheese room, and J.J. took out his books again.

But he couldn't work. He had to think of something to say to Jimmy. He couldn't just stand him up.

An idea came to him. It was so simple that he couldn't understand why it had taken so long to arrive. It would involve doing one of those jobs that were on the long finger, but if he left the history essay until tomorrow . . .

LAST NIGHT'S FUN

Trad

PART TWO

An hour later his puncture was fixed and he was just swinging up onto the saddle of his bike when he was spotted by Helen.

"J.J.!"

For a moment he pretended that he hadn't heard, but he couldn't hold out. He swung the bike round and skidded to a halt in front of her.

"Where you going?" she asked him.

"Just nipping down to see Jimmy."

"What about?"

"Nothing in particular."

Helen looked at her watch and J.J., in a reflex action, looked at his own. It was a fancy new one that he'd gotten for his birthday, with five different time zones and a calculator. It said four thirty.

"You'll be back for dinner?"

"'Course I will. There's loads of time."

J.J. began to move off again, but Helen called him back.

"Why don't you do me a favor and drop that cheese in to Anne Korff on your way?"

It wasn't on his way at all. Anne Korff lived in Doorus, about four miles southwest of the village. J.J. was about to point this out to Helen when he remembered her birthday wish. If it saved her time, he would do it. And the extra time on the road would give him a better chance to work out exactly what he was going to say to Jimmy.

But, oddly enough, he hadn't even gotten as far as the end of the drive before he knew. He would tell Jimmy the truth. With a bit of luck they would be able to get away from the thirty-two-inch television in Jimmy's sitting room and find somewhere quiet to talk. Then J.J. would level with him. Man-to-man stuff. "Look, Jimmy. It's like this. I want to go clubbing, I really do. But I want to play music more. It's in my blood. I was born to play, you know . . . ?"

If there was time he might go on to tell Jimmy why; let him in on some of the Liddy history. Not all of it, maybe. Not the bit about Helen's father and the fiddle. The rest, though. Then it would be up to Jimmy. If he really valued the friendship, he would understand. If he didn't, there wasn't much J.J. could do about it.

A new bank of dark clouds was rolling in from the west, but it was still dry. The bike was fast. It had had a puncture since the spring and now, flying along the autumn-colored lanes, J.J. found it hard to believe that he'd been without it for the whole summer for the sake of an hour's work or less. Perhaps that was part of the trick of dealing with this time deficit? Get the priorities right. If he'd had the bike during the summer he could have saved time for himself and for his parents. Maybe Helen's birthday present wouldn't turn out to be such a tall order after all. Ciaran had always taught him that anything was possible if you just managed to think about it in the right way.

He crossed the main road at the top end of the village and hurtled down through Croshua toward Doorus and the sea. The bike was a delight. Oxygen was pulsing through J.J.'s brain. He felt great.

Anne Korff was in her vegetable garden at the back of the house. She heard Lottie barking and came round to the front, cradling a bunch of carrots, two parsnips, and a dozen potatoes in her arms. J.J. offered her the cheese.

"You came down with it?" she said. "Ah, J.J., that was good of you. You shouldn't have."

"No problem." J.J. could see that Anne had no room in her hands to take the cheese. He opened the door for her, and she preceded him into the house.

"Would you believe that this is supposed to be my lunch?" she said. "Time these days. It just goes by like crazy."

She dumped the vegetables in the sink and rinsed her hands under the tap. J.J. put the cheese on top of her fridge.

"Be seeing you," he said, making for the door.

But Anne called him back. "Wait now. While you're here I have something to give you."

"No, no," said J.J. "There's no need."

"Not for bringing the cheese," said Anne. "I was thinking of you when I found it." She dried her hands on her jeans. "Now. Where is it?"

She began to rummage through the drawers and cupboards. J.J. fidgeted beside the door.

"What are you up to these days anyway?" she said.

"Oh, same old same old," said J.J. "School, hurling, music."

"A boy of many talents," said Anne. "Where the hell is that CD? I saw it a few days ago. Somewhere . . ." She moved to a different cupboard on the other side of the room. "Such a lot of junk. I need to sort myself out. There just isn't any time . . ."

"No," said J.J. "Any idea where I can buy some?"

Anne laughed. "I wish I knew. People use that expression so easily, don't you think? Buying time. It can't be done."

"Ah, it can, though," said J.J.

"Yes?" said Anne. "You know how?"

"Not yet. But I will."

"Oh?"

"Yep. That's what my mum wants for her birthday, and I plan to get it for her. Where there's a will there's a way."

Anne stopped rummaging and looked at J.J. Her face was thoughtful. "You really mean that?"

"Absolutely. One hundred percent. Whatever it takes, I'll do it."

"No, it's just . . ." Anne stopped herself. "Ach! It's too crazy."

"What's too crazy?"

"Nothing. I was just thinking that sometimes a person with so much determination can find a way to solve a problem that no one else can solve."

"What do you mean?" said J.J.

Anne began poking in the cupboard again, but J.J. could tell that her attention wasn't where her fingers were. "You've got an idea, haven't you?" he said. "I wish you'd tell me."

She sighed and closed the door of the cupboard. She gave him that thoughtful look again, as if she were appraising him.

"I have run out of ideas," she said. "That's the problem. I know where the time is going, but I don't know how to stop it. The situation is very serious, J.J. Much more serious than anyone realizes."

J.J. sat down on a stool. Jimmy could wait. Anne's words were creating an urgent tide in his blood. This mattered.

"Why? Where is it going?"

Anne seemed to be speaking as much to herself as to him. "A determined and talented young man. Perhaps that's what we need."

"I meant what I said, you know," said J.J. "I don't care what it takes. If I can buy time for my mum, I'll do it."

"I can see that you're determined," said Anne. "But I wonder if you're brave enough?"

"Brave enough? Why? What will I have to do?"

"You'll have to find out what the inside of a

souterrain looks like, for a start," said Anne. "If you have what it takes to go through, the rest of it might not be too bad."

"Go through where?"

"If I told you, you wouldn't believe me," said Anne. "If you're really sure you want to do this, I'll take you there. But after that you're on your own."

THE LAD THAT CAN
DO IT

Trad

The souterrain was a much greater test of J.J.'s courage than he had expected. The only way into it was to drop down into a hole in the ground, then lie down on your stomach and wriggle through a short tunnel. But once that was behind him J.J. didn't find it too bad. They had emerged into a long, narrow room with a muddy floor and an arched stone ceiling.

"Impressive, isn't it?" said Anne Korff, holding her candle up high so that J.J. could get a good look at the place.

"Yes," he said, and meant it.

"There used to be thousands of these all over Ireland," said Anne. "Very few are left now."

"What happened to them?"

"I suppose most of them are still there, somewhere. But people blocked them up."

"Why?"

"Well, I suppose they could have been dangerous. Maybe cattle fell into them, or children. Or perhaps there were people who didn't want anyone going in or out to the other side."

"You can get out the other side?" said J.J.

"That's what I'm going to show you," said Anne.

She led the way along the chamber and ducked through a second crawl hole in the wall at the end. J.J. followed the wavering light of her candle and found himself in a second room, slightly smaller than the first.

"Some of them have more chambers," said Anne. "This one has only two. Some parts of the world have amazingly complicated versions of this: pyramids, catacombs, henges, and suchlike. The Irish have always had a knack for keeping things simple."

J.J. could see no way out of the room. He began to get an inkling that "the other side" might not mean what he had assumed that it did. Anne led him into the farthest corner of the room. She indicated the angle where the two walls met.

"This is the way through," she said.

J.J. could see nothing but solid stone walls. "Where?"

"You really believe anything is possible?" said Anne.

"I do," said J.J. with conviction.

Anne Korff, carrying the only candle, walked through the wall and disappeared.

Suddenly alone, in impenetrable darkness, J.J. experienced a moment of gut-wrenching terror. But before he could yield to panic, Anne Korff came back, stepping out of the wall just as she had stepped into it.

"I'm going through now," she said. "And this time I'm not coming back. Do you want to come or stay?"

"Wait!" said J.J., too alarmed and confused to decide anything. "Don't leave me here in the dark again!"

"Come on, then," said Anne. "Don't think. Just walk . . ."

She caught hold of his sleeve. The prospect of being left alone in the darkness again was a lot more frightening than walking into a wall. As Anne stepped forward again, J.J. followed.

He had never imagined that it was possible to walk out of a place and arrive into it at the same time. But that appeared to be exactly what had happened. The room was exactly the same in every respect. The only difference that J.J. could perceive lay not in his surroundings but in himself. The sense of urgency that had pervaded his every waking minute for as long as he could remember was suddenly gone. He had grown so accustomed to it, in fact, that he had stopped being aware of it. Its sudden absence was astounding. He felt weightless.

Anne had turned back toward the wall. "It's a sort of membrane," she said, stretching out a hand. It disappeared into the stones. There was no gap. Nothing opened. The stones fitted snugly around her arm. They looked solid, but they must have been as fluid as water. "It's a perfect seal," she went on. "We don't break it when we come through. It molds itself around us and closes again behind us, just like water does when you get into it."

"Through where?" said J.J. He was still trying to get to grips with the concept of walking out of one room and arriving in it. As far as he could make out, they hadn't gone anywhere.

"Come and see."

Anne led the way through the two chambers; to J.J. it appeared to be the same way that they had come in. But when they emerged into the daylight, the world was not the way it had been when they left it. The sky that had been gray was blue. The fields and trees were no longer wearing their early autumn colors but were lush and green.

"I don't understand," said J.J.

"Welcome to Tír na n'Óg," said Anne Korff. "The land of eternal youth."

FAREWELL TO
IRELAND

Trad

J.J. sat on the warm, grassy bank of the ring fort, gazing up toward the sun-drenched mountains. "If it's as easy as that to get here," he said to Anne Korff, "why doesn't everybody do it?"

"Not so many people go into the souterrains anymore," said Anne. "And even when they do, it doesn't seem to occur to them to walk through the walls."

J.J. laughed. "I wonder why?" he said.

"People fall through occasionally," said Anne. "That's what happened to me. I was snooping around as usual. I dropped my flashlight and broke it. I tried to feel my way along the walls and the next thing I knew, I was here."

"Did you tell anyone about it then?"

Anne shook her head. "It was a long time before it

was clear to me what had happened. It's not easy to remember what happens during the time that you're here. When you go back it can be very confusing. Don't forget that, J.J. If you find yourself in a souterrain or anywhere else feeling very confused, don't be afraid. The mind goes into shock, that's all. Some of the memories usually come back later on. But by then . . . well, I don't know. I never felt like telling anyone I'd been to Tír na n'Óg. The chances are they wouldn't believe me. And what would happen if they did?"

She handed J.J. the candle and a box of matches. "You'll need these on your way back." She patted her jacket pocket. "I have more."

"Aren't you going to stay?"

"I would love to," said Anne, "but I have far too many things to do. Be sure and call in on me when you get home."

She walked back to the mouth of the souterrain, then turned back.

"J.J.?"

"Mmm?"

"Don't stay too long. Don't forget what happened to Oisín."

J.J. knew three people called Oisín. He couldn't see what relevance any of them had to his current situation.

"Oisín who?" he called. But Anne was already gone.

J.J. lay back in the grass. His watch said five thirty, but it was later than that here, judging by the position of the sun in the sky; closer to seven, he guessed. He would be late for dinner if he hung around too long, but for some reason he didn't feel remotely worried about it. He was on a mission, after all. Buying time was much more important in the long run. But he found that, hard as he tried, he couldn't work up any sense of urgency about that, either. In a nearby black-thorn bush a linnet was singing its heart out. J.J. couldn't understand how he had ever been so tyrannized by time. What had it all been about, all that racing around and getting nowhere? Even the thought of it made him feel exhausted. He yawned, sedated by the rasping of the crickets and the whistling of the birds. The sounds swelled to fill his head, then gradually faded out.

THE BIRD IN THE BUSH

Trad

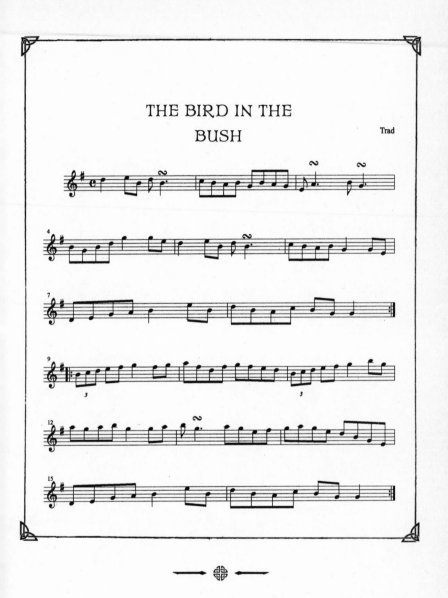

J.J. woke with a start. It felt to him as though he had slept for hours, but when he looked at his watch barely five minutes had passed. He'd only had forty winks.

He stretched out luxuriantly, a thing he hadn't done for years, and turned over onto his side to have another little snooze. He didn't need it, though. He was rested enough, and he was ready to get on with the business in hand. The sky was still blindingly bright, and he was looking forward to having a stroll around. There was never weather like this at home. Or perhaps there was, but everyone was too stressed out to enjoy it. A bit of sunshine; another commodity to be exploited—to make hay, or to get the house painted or to grab a quick swim on the way back from the supermarket.

He took off his jacket, slung it over his shoulder, and began to walk toward the village. Now that he was on the move, he discovered that this world was not nearly as similar to his own as he had first thought. There were fewer houses here, for one thing, and those there were didn't really look like houses at all. They had an irregular, organic appearance, as though they had been hewn out of chunks of rock, or been pushed up from beneath the ground by some gentle movement of the earth's crust. No people anywhere, not yet, though all the houses he passed had open doors and one had a small ginger cat sitting on its doorstep. There were, however, some rather strange bits of evidence that people did exist.

Socks.

When he passed the first one hanging from the hedgerow, J.J. paid it no attention. He'd often seen bits of clothing tangled up in hedges at home; it wasn't that unusual. But when he walked around a bend and found three more lying in the deep grass of the verge, and yet another one dangling from a branch a few meters farther on, he began to wonder about it.

There were more trees and bushes here, and more birds in them. There were fields, but their boundaries were ragged; their walls fallen down and their hedges full of gaps. The few cattle and horses he saw were fat and sleek, and wandered, as far as he could tell, wherever they pleased. Apart from them there was no sign of any kind of agriculture. There were no tractors, no black bales, no people out managing the land.

Where was everybody? And what kind of people lived in Tír na n'Óg anyway? Fairies? Leprechauns? Gods? He experienced a little shiver of apprehension, but it didn't swell into fear. The sun was too warm and bright, and besides, there were the socks. He was coming across them every hundred meters or so. One here, two or three there. There were tiny baby socks with cartoon characters or teddy bears on them; there were children's socks and adult socks, argyle socks and tartan socks and spotted socks, woollen socks and cotton socks and nylon socks. There were socks of every color and texture under the sun, and not a pair among them. Whoever they belonged to, J.J. decided, could not be too frightening.

It ought to have taken him at least half an hour to walk to the village from where he started out, but when he got to the main road his watch was still saying five thirty-five. He shook it and held it up to his ear. Silence. A single tick. More silence. He pressed all the buttons, trying all the different time zones, pulling and pushing on the tiny dials that set the hands and the alarm. Nothing made any difference. He could see the second hand moving, but absurdly slowly; a single, jerky step, then nothing, then another one. J.J. tried to work up some annoyance at it, but he couldn't. What did it matter if his watch had stopped? What was the rush, anyway?

He walked on, and arrived at the edge of the village. His village. It was certainly Kinvara, but at the same time it wasn't. A pair of metal water pumps, painted yellow and blue, stood where MacMahon's filling station ought to be. Opposite it, the same line of sturdy trees leaned over the high stone wall, but behind them, in place of the church, was a massive outcrop of gray rock with circles and spirals carved into its walls. Scrubby bushes and ferns grew out of its crevices. J.J. moved on, preferring not to dwell upon who, or what, might be worshipped in such an edifice.

The same streets ran through the village in the same directions. It had the same corners and crossroads as far as he could see, but the streets were cobbled instead of paved, and the houses that lined them were similar to those he had already passed. They leaned against one another at all kinds of odd angles, not one of them in proper alignment with its neighbor, but all of them somehow relaxed and comfortable with the arrangements. All of them, as far as J.J. could ascertain, were empty. Where was everyone?

J.J. listened. There was no wind. He caught glimpses of the sea as he passed the side streets that ran down to it at right angles to the main street, but he couldn't hear it. Its surface was like glass. The air was too still for there to be any waves. But he could, or he imagined he could, hear something else. The faint strains of music drifting up the street toward him.

He walked on, heading toward it. As he did so, he saw a movement in the shadows against the wall. A large gray dog that he hadn't noticed before stood up. It was directly in J.J.'s path. He crossed to the other side of the street, but the dog moved out from the wall to intercept his path. Even from a distance he could see that the creature was in a very bad way. It was walking on three legs. The fourth, one of the hind legs, was partially severed at the hock, and what was left of it was dragging along behind. J.J. shuddered. The dreadful sight cast the first damper on his experience of Tír na n'Óg and made him wonder what other horrors it might be holding in store for him.

He stopped in the middle of the street. The dog was huge. Its wiry coat and long, fine muzzle gave it the appearance of an Irish wolfhound, but it was much broader and heavier than any J.J. had seen. He watched as it approached, ready to run if it showed any hint of aggression. It didn't. Its demeanor was benign; almost servile. J.J. stood his ground and waited as it came right up to him and sniffed at his hand. Then he reached out and stroked its head.

The injury, when J.J. bent down to inspect it more closely, was truly horrendous. The lower part of the leg was hanging on by a thin cord of skin and sinew. Bone showed through on both parts of the leg. A drop of blood fell from it and soaked into the dust.

"You poor thing," said J.J. "What on earth happened to you?"

As if in answer, the dog suddenly pricked its ears and turned to look back down the street. A brown goat was tearing up toward them, closely followed by a large, bearded man.

"Stop her!" he yelled at J.J.

J.J. spread his arms and barred the goat's path. She dodged to the left, but J.J. was well accustomed to goat behavior and had anticipated her. Again he barred her path, and this time she checked and doubled back, straight into the arms of her pursuer.

"Good man," he said. "She's an awful wagon, so she is."

The goat let out a plaintive bleat and struggled, but the man had a firm grip on one of her horns and he wasn't about to lose her again. "Come on down to the quay," he said to J.J. "Everybody's down there."

"I just found this dog," said J.J.

"Oh, yes," said the man. "That's Bran."

"She's had an awful accident," said J.J.

"'Twas a fight, I'd say," said the man. "Poor old Bran."

He began to walk back down the hill, dragging the struggling goat behind him.

"We can't just leave her," said J.J.

"Don't mind her," said the man. "She'll probably follow us down."

J.J. watched him as he turned the bend in the street and went out of sight. He was standing just a few feet away from the vet's office, but it looked, in this Kinvara, just like an ordinary house. He glanced across the street to where Séadna Tobín's pharmacy would have been standing in his world. It seemed a bit more hopeful. Perhaps someone there could tell him where to find the vet?

The door, like all the doors in the street, stood wide open. J.J. stood beside it and listened. There were people in there, somewhere at the very back of the shop. They seemed to be having an argument, though, from the sound of it, and J.J. was reluctant to knock. Perhaps the best thing would be to go down to the quay and see if there was anyone there who could help.

THE BIG BOW-WOW

Trad

"Did you pass J.J. on the road?" Helen asked Phil when he arrived for the céilí.

"No," said Phil. "Isn't he here?"

Helen shook her head. "He'll probably be here in a minute."

Phil unlatched his case and took out the guitar. "I didn't track down our policeman either," he said. "No one seems to know where he lives. I suppose he hasn't been here long enough."

Helen glanced toward the door. Her mind was not on the policeman. "Shame," she said.

"We're sure to run into him before the next one," said Phil. "If he turns up in Green's again I'll give you a shout, will I?"

"Worth a try, I suppose," said Helen.

"The next time he comes with his fiddle, that is," said Phil. "Not the next time he takes our names."

The dancers were drifting in, two or three at a time, and wandering toward the makeshift bar. Helen put down the concertina and made her way over to the door. Night had fallen. She looked out into the dark yard, already full of parked cars. Another group of dancers was arriving.

"You didn't pass J.J. on the road, I suppose?" she asked them.

Anne Korff had just finished letting the air out of J.J.'s front tire when the phone rang. By her watch it was nearly ten o'clock. She lifted the receiver. It was, as she had suspected it might be, Helen Liddy. Anne listened, then said, "Yes. He dropped in the cheese, but that was a good while ago now. Maybe five o'clock or so."

"Did he say where he was going?"

"I don't think so," said Anne, quite truthfully. "He was mostly concerned with your birthday present."

"My birthday present?"

"Something he wanted to buy for you."

"Oh," said Helen. "He said he was going to see

Jimmy Dowling, but there's no answer there. Maybe he called in on someone else."

"Maybe," said Anne. "He left his bike here, you know. It had a puncture. I offered to give him a lift, but he said he wouldn't take it."

"Oh, maybe that's it," said Helen. She sounded relieved. "He's probably getting a lift up with someone."

She rang off, and Anne sat down heavily on the nearest chair. Distressing J.J.'s parents hadn't been part of the plan. Now that she thought about it, there hadn't really been a plan at all. She should probably go and get J.J. back before Helen got any more worried. But on the other hand, if J.J. did somehow succeed in getting her the birthday present she had asked for, she would be more than compensated. Perhaps a bit longer wouldn't do too much harm.

Helen returned to the céilí. The dancers were still standing around the bar, waiting for the music to start. Marian, who was always in big demand as a dancing partner, disengaged herself from the set that had nabbed her and came over.

"You all right, Mum?"

"I'm just worried about J.J."

"Don't," said Marian. "He's well able to look after himself. He won't do anything stupid."

"I suppose so," said Helen. "I just can't understand where he could be."

"Didn't he tell you?" said Marian. "The rotten sod."

"Tell me what?"

"He's gone clubbing in Gort."

"Clubbing?"

"Yeah. They had it all planned. He's staying the night at Jimmy Dowling's house. I can't believe he just went. He promised me he'd tell you."

THE EAVESDROPPER

Trad

The dog limped painfully behind J.J. as he walked down toward the quay. At the foot of the hill the main street formed one edge of an open triangular area. The second side was another row of squodgy houses, and the third was the harbor wall. In this space, the residents of the village had gathered together to dance beneath the open sky.

To J.J.'s disappointment, they appeared to be neither leprechauns nor gods. The clothes they were wearing were representative of the changing fashions of several centuries, giving J.J. the vague impression that he had stumbled upon some kind of fancy dress party. Other than that the people on the quay appeared little different from the population of any Irish village.

The doors of the three nearest pubs were open. In his village they were called Green's, Connolly's and Sexton's, but here they had no names; not written above their doors, anyway. Those people who were not dancing lounged against their walls or sat on benches or on the curb of the footpath, holding goblets and tankards, and pint glasses of what looked to J.J. suspiciously like draft Guinness.

No one took any notice of him. The dog detached herself from him and parked herself on the footpath between the wall of Connolly's and the arrangement of chairs, barrels, and upturned buckets where the musicians were seated. J.J. leaned against the corner and observed them from behind. There were six of them: two fiddlers, a piper, a whistle and a flute player, and, playing the bodhrán, the bearded man that J.J. had encountered chasing the goat. They were in the middle of a set of reels. J.J. knew the tune they were playing, or a version of it, but he couldn't think of its name. They weren't playing particularly fast, but the rhythm, the lift in the music was electrifying. It made J.J.'s feet itch to dance.

The dancers didn't form sets, like they did at the Liddy céilís, but nor did they dance alone, like the step or sean nós dancers at fleadhs. In some way the whole gathering contrived to dance both separately and together, interacting with one another now and again, then disengaging to form part of the bigger, and somehow perfectly circular, whole. Their footwork was spectacular; both energetic and graceful. Their bodies seemed to be as light as air.

Far too soon for J.J. the set of tunes came to an end. The dancers drifted apart, laughing, adjusting their clothing or their hair. Some of them made for the pubs, others stood around and talked or flirted with one another. Some of the musicians got up as well, and as they did so they noticed him leaning against the wall. There was a brief discussion among them, then one of the fiddle players, a fair-haired young man with a winning smile, beckoned to him.

"You're welcome," he said, guiding J.J. into an empty seat. "I haven't seen you around here before."

"I haven't been here before," said J.J.

"You're all the more welcome, so," said the fiddler. "We don't see many new faces. What's your name?"

"J.J."

The young man introduced the musicians. The piper was called Cormac, the whistle and flute players were Jennie and Marcus, and the bodhrán player, the goat chaser, was Devaney. The other fiddle player, who didn't shake J.J.'s hand because she appeared to be asleep, was called Maggie.

"And I'm Aengus," the fiddler finished up. "Do you play yourself?"

"I do, a bit," said J.J. "Fiddle mostly. A small bit on the flute."

"Great stuff," said Aengus. "You might play a tune with us."

"Ah, no." J.J. was not normally shy to play, but the music he had heard here was subtly different in its rhythms and intonations. He would like to hear more before he picked up an instrument and tried to join in. Besides, he remembered with an effort, he had not come here to play tunes.

"I came across this dog in the street. Do you know who she belongs to?"

All the musicians turned and looked at the dog, which was now stretched at full length along the footpath.

"That's Bran," said Jennie.

"Is she yours?"

"She isn't anyone's," said Jennie.

"Someone ought to take her to the vet," said J.J. "I don't mind doing it if no one else will." He only had ten euros on him and he knew that wouldn't pay a vet's bill, but he would cross that bridge if and when he came to it.

"There's nothing anyone can do for Bran, J.J.," said Aengus. "You shouldn't concern yourself with her."

"Come and play a tune," said Marcus.

J.J. was horrified by everyone's attitude toward the dog. He wasn't sentimental himself; he had grown up around farm animals and had seen them with all kinds of damage. But Bran's injuries were particularly awful. They needed attention.

"I didn't come here to play tunes," he said, a bit more irritably than he meant to.

"Oh?" J.J. thought he glimpsed a corresponding gleam of antagonism in Aengus's clear green eyes, but if he did, it vanished as quickly as it had arisen. "What did you come here for, then? A rescue mission for lame dogs?"

"No," said J.J.

"You have another reason for being here, so," said Maggie, who wasn't asleep after all.

"I have, I suppose," said J.J., although the business with the dog had almost driven it out of his mind. It seemed absurd now, as he said it. "I was told you might be able to help me buy some time."

"Time?" said Devaney.

"No bother," said Aengus.

"We've heaps of it," said Cormac, "and we've no use for it at all."

"Oh, great," said J.J., though it all seemed even more absurd now. "Will you sell me some, then?"

"Take it," said Aengus. "Take it all."

J.J. was silent, trying to make sense of what he was hearing.

"We don't want it," Aengus went on. "You're welcome to it."

"You mean . . ." said J.J. "You mean . . . just take it?"

"Just take it," said Aengus.

J.J. looked around at the other faces, wondering what kind of joke was being played on him. There was no sign that he could see of any malice or amusement. But it couldn't possibly be as simple as it appeared to be.

Devaney sensed that he was in difficulty. "Wait, now," he said. "Maybe it would be better if he gave us something for it."

"It would," said Maggie. "It would cement the deal."

"And he would have more value on it, that way," said Marcus.

"Right, so," said Aengus. "Make us an offer for the lot."

J.J. felt the ten-euro note in his pocket. If he'd known he was going to be in this situation he would have come better prepared. He wished he'd had the foresight to ask Anne Korff for a loan.

He took it out. "This is all I have on me."

They all stared at the shabby note in his hand. It was a mistake, he knew. He had insulted them.

"I can get more," he said hastily. "I have a couple of hundred in the credit union."

"Ah, no," said Cormac. "It isn't that."

"You could wave any amount of that stuff around in front of us," said Jennie.

"It's no use to us," said Maggie.

"We don't use it," said Devaney.

"Have you nothing else?" said Aengus.

J.J. searched his pockets. In the inside breast pocket of his jacket he had the candle and matches that Anne Korff had given him. He needed them for his way back. His penknife was in there as well, but he was very attached to it. If he had to he might offer it, but it would have to be a last resort. He searched his other pockets.

Aengus looked up at the sky. Devaney examined his

drum skin and gave it a couple of hefty clouts. Maggie appeared to go to sleep again.

"There must be something," said Devaney.

"I'm sure there is, if we could think of it," said Jennie.

"There is," said Aengus. "There's something we all want."

"What?" said J.J.

"'Dowd's Number Nine.'"

"Yes!" said Maggie, who wasn't asleep after all.

"Good thinking," said Cormac.

J.J. racked his brains. It was a common enough tune—so common, in fact, that there were endless jokes about its name. There was no "Dowd's Number Eight" or "Dowd's Number Ten," no "Dowd's Number One" or "Two," or any other numbers at all. Just "Dowd's Number Nine."

J.J. knew he played it. It was one of Helen's favorite tunes. There were dozens, possibly hundreds of tunes that J.J. could play if they came up in a session, but the problem was that he seldom remembered their names. Unless he was playing in a competition it never seemed important to him.

"Don't you know it?" said Aengus, sounding disappointed.

"I do," said J.J. "I just can't think of it. How does it start?"

"That's what we want to know," said Maggie.

"We used to have it, all of us," said Marcus. "It slipped our minds. We'd love to get it back."

"It's a great tune," said Devaney.

"One of the best," said Jennie.

J.J. thought hard. The tune was associated with Joe Cooley, the great South Galway accordion player. It was on the album that had been recorded during a pub session shortly before he died. Helen had it on in the house constantly. J.J. knew it backward.

Aengus offered him the fiddle. J.J. took it, thought about the CD, tried a tune.

"That's 'The Blackthorn Stick,'" said Devaney.

J.J. tried another.

"'The Skylark,'" said Maggie.

J.J. wrung his memory again, but nothing else would come to him. "I have some nice Paddy Fahy tunes," he said. "I could teach you one of those."

Jennie giggled. Aengus shook his head. "We have all Paddy's tunes," he said.

"He got them from us, actually," said Cormac.

"He wouldn't like to hear you say that," said J.J.

"Why wouldn't he?" said Aengus. "He'd be the first

to admit it if he thought anyone would believe him."

J.J. wasn't sure, but he wasn't about to argue the point. "I got a nice jig the other day," he said.

"Let's hear it," said Aengus.

J.J. started to play his great-grandfather's jig. After the first couple of bars the others joined in. J.J. was about to stop, since it was obvious that they knew the tune, but it was lovely playing with them. Once through the tune and he was beginning to hear the accents and slurs that gave their playing its distinctive lift. By the third time through he was beginning to adopt it into his own bowing. He caught Maggie's eye and changed to the second of the tunes that Helen had taught him the night before. The others knew that one, too. When it came to an end, Aengus took back the fiddle.

"You're a lovely player," he said. "But you would wear out the hairs on my bow before you came up with a tune that we didn't know."

"They all come from this side," said Marcus.

That was what the old people had believed. Could it be that they were right? But not all the tunes, surely. Paddy Fahy wasn't the only composer of new tunes. There were loads of others.

"I wrote a tune myself once," said J.J.

"You didn't," said Maggie. "You just think you did."

"You heard us playing it," said Devaney, "and you thought you were hearing it inside of your own head."

"It happens to lots of people," said Jennie.

"Play it," said Aengus.

J.J. lifted the fiddle and played the first few notes. The others were on to it in a flash. J.J. stopped and handed back the fiddle.

"I don't believe it," he said. "It isn't even a good tune."

"Not all of them are," said Maggie.

"If it was," said Marcus, "someone else would have taken the trouble to steal it from us long before you did."

"Ah, now," said Aengus. "We don't consider it stealing."

There was a small silence, broken by a faint bleat that J.J. thought came from the bodhrán. Devaney clouted it a few times, which appeared to shut it up. J.J. looked around for the goat. There was no sign of it. His attention returned to the matter of "Dowd's Number Nine."

"No other tunes you've forgotten, I suppose?" he said.

They all shook their heads.

"I tell you what," said Maggie. "Why don't you take the time anyway? You can owe us 'Dowd's Number Nine.'"

"Brilliant," said Aengus, and all the others agreed enthusiastically.

"Great," said J.J. "I'll learn it from Mum and come back with it."

"And if you don't," said Cormac, "can't one of us come over and get it from you?"

"No," said Maggie. "We tried that before, don't you remember?"

"So we did," said Cormac.

"That's the trouble with going over to the other side," said Devaney. "As soon as you get there, you forget what it was you were looking for."

"I won't forget," said J.J. "I'll write it down on my hand. I'll bring it back."

"Mighty," said Marcus,

"Sorted," said Maggie.

"Off you go, so," said Aengus. "Take all the time you want."

J.J. stood up, delighted with himself. The others stood up as well, putting down their instruments and shaking hands on the deal.

"OK," J.J. said. "So how do I take it?"

"Don't you know?" said Maggie.

"No," said J.J. expectantly.

One by one the others sat down again.

"Nor do we," said Devaney.

"I thought there might be a catch," said Aengus.

DROWSY MAGGIE

Trad

PART THREE

Helen was angry with J.J. If she hadn't been, she might not have left it until dinnertime the following evening before she rang the Dowlings to find out if and when he was planning to come home. When she discovered that he wasn't there and hadn't been clubbing either, she flew into a panic. She interrogated Marian until she reduced her to tears, then phoned around to all J.J.'s current and former friends. No one had seen him.

"Perhaps it's a girl?" said Ciaran.

"He's only fifteen!" said Helen.

"So what? So were Romeo and Juliet."

"He hasn't eloped, Ciaran!" Helen snapped.

"There's no need to take it out on us!" Ciaran snapped back. "He'll probably walk in that door any moment with a perfectly rational explanation for where he's been."

They all agreed that he probably would, but the conviction didn't last long. Marian blamed herself for telling Helen that he'd gone clubbing. Helen blamed herself for leaving it so late to ring the Dowlings. Ciaran got tired of listening to them both blaming themselves and went for a drive around the village. He was certain that he'd find J.J. there, or on the road home. But when he came back without him, Helen's optimism had run out.

"This just isn't J.J.'s style," she said. "I'm sure something has happened to him. I'm calling the police."

Sergeant Early took Helen's call. She gave him the background to what had happened and a description of J.J. and the clothes he had been wearing when they'd last seen him. He promised to send the details out to all the officers in the area. An hour later he arrived at the house and took fuller statements from all three of them. He made a particular point of enquiring about J.J.'s state of mind. Was he happy at school? Did he have friends? A girlfriend? Had he ever taken a drink or, to their knowledge, any kind of drugs? Had he had a disagreement with any of them before he left?

When he had finished, he closed the notepad and

put away his pen. "I'd try not to worry too much if I were you," he said. "Ninety-five percent of people reported missing turn up within forty-eight hours." On the front doorstep he hesitated. "This house is famous for its music," he went on. "I heard your mother play many's the time, and yourself as well, Mrs. Liddy."

Helen ignored the "Mrs." "Music runs in the family all right," she said.

"I play a bit myself," said Sergeant Early. "Banjo. I couldn't live without it."

"I know how you feel," said Helen.

As he closed the door behind him, Ciaran said, "Jaysus. Can you believe it? They're all at it. The Garda Síochána Céilí Band!"

The sergeant's reassurances had done little to allay Helen's fears. There had been two disappearances from the Liddy house in as many generations, and on neither occasion had the missing person turned up. The sergeant's questions about J.J.'s mental health had put worse thoughts into Ciaran's head. The rate of teenage suicides in the country was soaring. While Helen started the milking and Marian listened for the phone, he made a quiet, thorough search of every building on the farm.

THE ONE THAT WAS LOST

Paddy O'Brien

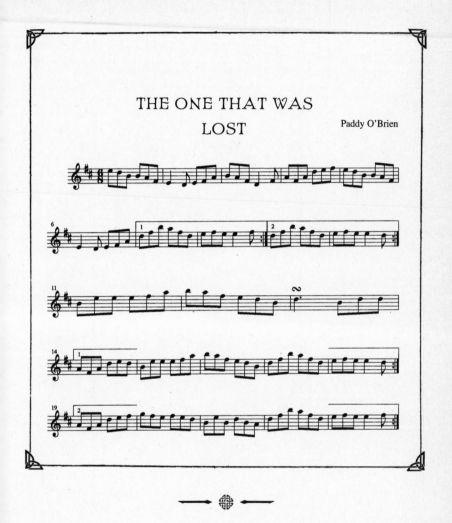

For some reason that was not at all clear to J.J., the party had come to an end and people were wandering off in each of the three available directions.

"Maybe they didn't like my tunes," he said.

"Why wouldn't they?" said Marcus.

Devaney was struggling with the bodhrán, doing something with a small wrench. The drum, as far as J.J. could ascertain, appeared to be resisting the process and was emitting loud, goaty bawls. Despite the racket, Maggie had dropped off to sleep again.

J.J. watched Devaney for a while, trying to work out what was going on. "Anyway," he said, "I don't see why you're so keen to get rid of your time. I wish I had half as much of it."

"We don't want it," said Maggie, without opening her eyes.

"We don't want any time at all," said Jennie.

"It's a mistake," said Aengus. "Something has gone wrong. It shouldn't be here."

J.J. was beginning to think the whole thing was some kind of elaborate wind-up, engineered by Anne Korff.

"What would you do without time?" he asked.

"Live," said Maggie.

"Things have already started dying," said Cormac.

"What?" said J.J.

"Look," said Cormac. He pointed to a black speck on the floor underneath Jennie's chair. J.J. bent to examine it. It was a dead fly.

"That usedn't to happen," said Cormac.

J.J. laughed incredulously. "You should see my house," he said. "It's crawling with dead flies. Well. Not exactly crawling, but—"

"And so it should be," said Maggie, her eyes opening again. "But it shouldn't happen here."

"This is Tír na n'Óg," said Aengus. "The land of eternal youth. But that fly got old. It got old and then it died. That oughtn't to happen."

Devaney thumped the bodhrán with the wrench and the struggle, for the moment at least, ended.

"We have a desperate problem," he said.

"It's called time," said Maggie.

Aengus looked up at the sky, as he had done several times since J.J. had arrived. "You see the sun?"

"I do," said J.J. "It's lovely, isn't it?"

"It is," said Aengus. He pointed to a spot in the sky, almost overhead. "But it used to be there."

"Of course it did," said J.J. "And later on it will be there"—he pointed to the west, above the horizon—"and after that it will go down."

"That's what we don't want," said Devaney.

"But . . ."

Aengus pointed upward again. "That's where the sun belongs. In this world."

"What? Always?" said J.J.

Maggie sighed wearily. "We never used to have any 'always,'" she said. "There was only ever 'now.'"

"Something's gone dreadfully wrong," said Aengus. "That's why we were hoping you'd take it away with you."

"Back where it belongs," said Cormac.

"And good riddance to it," said Devaney.

J.J. had gone beyond disbelief and was slipping toward cynicism. "What I don't understand," he said, "is why you've all been playing tunes and dancing all afternoon. If your problem is as serious as you say it is, why aren't you trying to do something about it?"

"He has a point," said Jennie.

"He does," said Maggie.

"The truth is," said Aengus, "we're not very good at worrying about things."

"We haven't had much practice," said Devaney.

"Lucky you," said J.J. "I could give you a few lessons."

"Great," said Aengus.

At that moment the bodhrán started banging and bleating wildly. Devaney picked up the wrench, then changed his mind and put it down again. He stood up and hurled the bodhrán out into the middle of the empty street. As it touched the ground, it turned into the brown goat that he had been chasing up the road when J.J. first encountered him.

J.J. stared at it. He could take all the nonsense about dead flies and eternal youth with a pinch of salt, but he had just seen something happen that was impossible. The goat shook herself, recovered her dignity, and wandered away along the quay.

"Can we start now?" Aengus was saying.

"Hmm?" said J.J.

"Worrying lessons," said Aengus. "Can we start them now?"

THE SETTING SUN

Trad

"Well," said J.J. He was still stunned by what he had seen on the quay and was having difficulty marshaling his thoughts. "I suppose . . . I mean . . . you don't really worry on purpose."

He was walking up the main street of the village with Aengus, who wanted to get some tobacco.

"No?" said Aengus.

"No. You just think about something that's a problem and it just happens."

"There must be more to it than that," said Aengus.

They were outside the pharmacy, and J.J. stopped to have a look in the window. It was full of ancient bottles and jars and boxes. A row of little brass buckets offered powders of different colors, and one was full to the brim of a shining liquid that looked to

J.J. as if it might be mercury. In the dark recesses of the shop he could just make out more odd goods: pestles and mortars, globes, brass beakers engraved with unknown scripts. J.J. smiled to himself. Séadna Tobín, the man who ran the pharmacy in the other Kinvara, would get a great laugh out of this.

"What are all these things?" he asked Aengus.

"Ingredients," said Aengus. "For alchemy."

"What's alchemy?"

"The art of making gold."

"Really?" said J.J. "You can make gold out of these things?"

"I don't think so," said Aengus. "But I don't suppose there's any harm in trying."

"Can we go in?" said J.J.

"No, no." Aengus took him by the elbow and steered him clear of the doorway. "It's full of leprechauns. You don't want to get mixed up with them."

"Why not?"

"Tricky little people," said Aengus. "But pure mad about gold."

"So they're the ones who buy this stuff?"

"They are."

J.J. looked in the window again. "How do they

pay for it if you don't use money?"

"They pay with gold."

"Eh?" said J.J. "Where's the sense in that?"

"No point in asking me," said Aengus. "I never did get a grip on the concept of profit."

Inside the shop a number of shrill little voices embarked upon an angry argument. As J.J. followed Aengus away from the window, he noticed that the dog had followed them. She limped up to him and he rubbed her ears.

"What happened to her?" he asked Aengus.

"I don't know," said Aengus. "She was like that when she appeared."

"Appeared from where?"

"From the other side. Your side."

"But why doesn't anyone do something about her? She must belong to somebody. Surely?"

"She does," said Aengus. "She belongs to Fionn Mac Cumhail."

"Fionn Mac Cumhail? But he's not real. He's just a character in a story."

"Not at all," said Aengus. "He's as real as you or me."

"I suppose he might have been once," said J.J., "but it must have been an awful long time ago. How old does that make the dog?"

Aengus shrugged. "How would I know? Can you tell from her teeth?"

"That's not what I mean," said J.J. "If she was Fionn Mac Cumhail's dog, she must be ancient. Hundreds and hundreds of years old. When did she appear?"

Aengus looked up at the sky again and pointed. "When the sun was there," he said. "And now, if you don't mind, I have to nip in and get that tobacco."

He went into Burke's shop, or what would have been Burke's in J.J.'s version of the village. It didn't look like a shop now. All he could see through the window was a few old wooden shelves covered in ivy. He was about to follow Aengus in when the dog shoved her head up under his hand again, looking for more sympathy. He scratched her under the chin and bent to look at the wound. Another drop of blood fell from it, and another. Whatever that nonsense was about Fionn Mac Cumhail, the wound was still fresh. A good vet would almost certainly be able to do something about it. But were there any vets here?

J.J. walked back along the street, and Bran hobbled at his heels. At the square he crossed over to the house that ought to have been the vet's practice. He knocked on the door anyway. If Burke's was a shop, and if the chemist's was an alchemist's, then perhaps there might be some version of a vet in the house. But the door was opened by Drowsy Maggie.

"Hello again," she said. "Have you come for a tune?"

"No," said J.J. "I was looking for the vet."

"What's a vet?"

"A vet. You know. A doctor for animals."

"I didn't know there was such a thing," said Maggie. "We don't have them here, anyway. Nor doctors, either."

"You don't have doctors?"

"What would we want them for?"

"To make you better," said J.J. "When you're ill."

Maggie shook her head. "It doesn't work like that here. If you're well you're well and you won't get ill. If you're ill you're ill and you won't get any better. I wouldn't worry about her. Nobody gets any worse, either . . ." Maggie hesitated. "At least, that's the way it was"—she pointed at the sky—"when the sun was where it ought to be."

J.J.'s head was beginning to spin. "But she's in pain," he said.

"She is, isn't she?" said Maggie. "Poor Bran. Are you sure you don't fancy a tune?"

THE GOLD RING

Trad

The new policeman arrived into work bright and early on Monday morning. He was sent, along with Garda Treacy, to make house-to-house calls along the route that the missing boy would have taken between Anne Korff's house and the village. To Larry's relief, Anne Korff herself was not at home. He had, during the journey from Gort, already referred to her once as "Lucy Campbell," and he didn't want any further confusions arising.

They brought a photograph of J.J. with them and showed it to everyone they found at home that morning, but no one remembered seeing the boy on Saturday. One or two people, however, had seen Garda O'Dwyer. After the second reference to his beautiful fiddle playing, Garda Treacy said, "We must get a listen to you sometime. Where do you play?"

"At home, mostly," said Larry.

"Does Sergeant Early know?"

"I don't think so," said Larry.

Treacy stopped the car outside the next house on the road, but he didn't get out. "He plays himself, you know. The banjo."

"A monstrous instrument," said Larry. "They should have left it in America where it belongs."

"Don't let the sergeant hear you say that," said Treacy.

"I won't," said Larry.

They returned to the station for their lunch, and afterward they drove to the village to continue with their inquiries. They started with the shops. Word of J.J.'s disappearance had reached everyone by that time, and the two guards met with a lot of concern, but no information.

They were in Fallon's supermarket when they ran into Thomas O'Neill, one of Kinvara's oldest residents. He was buying milk and had already paid for it, but he stayed beside the cash desk when the two guards came in. He listened as Garda Treacy began to interview the girl who was at the till, then he stepped up close to Garda O'Dwyer.

"I know you from somewhere," he said.

"Really?" said Larry, smiling benignly and edging away at the same time. He had a horror of old people, especially those with good memories.

"We've met," said Thomas. "I can't think where."

"I can't think where either," said Larry. "But people often mistake me for someone else. I'm told I'm the spit of my father when he was my age."

"What's your name?"

Larry told him. Thomas shook his head. "It's ringing no bells," he said. "Where are you from?"

"I grew up in Sligo," said Larry. "But I've moved around a lot."

Garda Treacy was moving toward the door and Larry made to join him.

"It'll come to me," said Thomas.

"We're looking for a missing teenager," said Larry. He showed Thomas the photograph. "Perhaps you saw him on Saturday evening?"

"I know the lad well," said Thomas, "but I don't recall seeing him on Saturday."

"If you think of anything, give us a ring," said Larry, and made his escape.

The day flew by as rapidly for the two policemen as for the rest of the population. All the same, Larry was tired and footsore by the end of it. All he could think about was getting home.

"What do you think?" said Treacy as they left the barracks.

"About what?" said Larry.

"About the boy? I'd say he's just off on a jaunt somewhere."

"He is, I'd say," said Larry.

"They don't give a toss, the young lads these days. Worrying their parents and wasting our time at the public's expense."

"What can you do?" said Larry.

Treacy shrugged. "Have you any plans for tonight?"

"A hot bath and an early night," said Larry. "I can't wait to get home."

"There's a trivia night in Labane," said Treacy. "We're one short of a team."

Larry shook his head. "I'd be useless. Half the time I can't even remember my own name."

IT'LL COME TO ME

Kate Thompson

"In your far distant history," said Aengus, "people moved freely between the two worlds."

They were sitting on the curb, and Aengus was struggling with the plastic wrapping on a new packet of pipe tobacco.

"Then there was this humongous battle between your lot and our lot."

"Who are your lot?" said J.J.

"In those days you used to call us Danu's people; the Tuatha de Danaan. It was a long time afterward that you started calling us fairies."

"So you are fairies?"

"We're people," said Aengus, "but you can call us what you like. There isn't really a forum for raising an objection, you know?" He put on a lager-lout voice. *"Oi, you. Who are you calling a fairy?"*

J.J. laughed. Aengus was still struggling with the plastic; all thumbs. "Anyway, we had magic on our side—"

"Magic?"

"Just a bit. But your lot had strength of numbers and . . . well . . . the truth is they had better leadership than we did. We hadn't really much of a notion of what we were doing. We've never been much use in your world." He succeeded in getting the plastic off and began to fumble with the foil wrapping inside it. "For some reason that I've never been able to fathom, there seems to be a limit to the number of people we can turn into pigs."

"Pigs?" said J.J.

"At any given time, that is," said Aengus. "One or two at a time seems to be the most we can do. It doesn't work with armies."

"You're having me on," said J.J., although even as he spoke he remembered Devaney and the bodhrán and he wasn't so sure. "You can't really turn people into pigs, can you?"

"No bother," said Aengus. "Anything at all, for that matter." He stuffed a small clay pipe with tobacco and lit it with a purple lighter, then went on. "Some of your storybooks suggest we lost the war, but that isn't right. Well, maybe it's a little bit right. In any event, there was a settlement. We were allowed to go home to Tír na n'Óg as long as we stayed here and never went over into your world again."

"That doesn't make sense to me," said J.J. "Why would our side choose to stay in my world and die if they could have eternal youth?"

"They never trusted this world," said Aengus, puffing furiously at the pipe. "And they wanted time. They wanted to have pasts and futures. They wanted the ability to shape their world and to accumulate wealth and power. Christianity had just arrived, so they weren't so worried about dying, now that they could look forward to an afterlife."

"Is there an afterlife, then?" said J.J.

Aengus shrugged. "I don't know," he said. "Why should I care?"

In J.J.'s mind one of a whole heap of pennies began to drop. "So," he said carefully, "if we have living and dying and all that stuff and you don't, does that mean that you're . . . you know . . . immortal?"

"Not even remotely," said Aengus. "I'm as mortal as you are. The only difference between you and me is that you have forgotten how to use magic. If you were born here you'd be the same as me. It's the worlds that are different, not us. Yours has time. Ours doesn't." He glanced up at the sky. "At least," he said, "it didn't. Until the leak started."

J.J. tried to absorb the information. It was an awful lot for a teenager, even a talented one, to get his head around. "You're trying to tell me that time is leaking out of our world into yours?"

"Exactly," said Aengus.

"So that's why we never have enough of it?"

"Spot on."

"And you have too much."

"Way too much."

"My God," said J.J. "We have to do something about it. Where is the leak?"

"That's the problem," said Aengus. "We have no idea."

THE FAIRY HORNPIPE

Trad

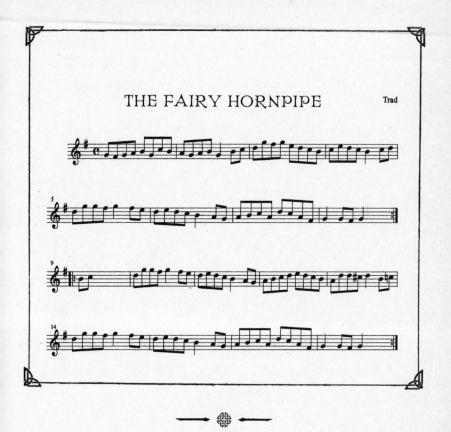

J.J. was charged with energy. The languid feeling that he'd been enjoying since he emerged from the souterrain was gone, along with the mental woolliness that had accompanied it. All the nonsense that he'd been hearing had suddenly become clear, like a fuzzy image pulled into sharp focus.

"Okay," said J.J. "For thousands of years—our years, that is—the two worlds have been perfectly sealed from each other."

"By the time skin," said Aengus. "The fluid wall between the worlds."

"And now," said J.J., "all of a sudden, there's a leak."

"We've checked all the obvious places on both sides," said Aengus. "Some of us have been over to your world, and we have one or two people like Anne

Korff who are still searching over there. The thing is, there aren't many places where there is two-way traffic. Most of the souterrains are blocked on one side or the other."

"What do you mean by two-way traffic?" said J.J.

"The souterrains are for your benefit, not ours," said Aengus. "We can go through pretty much anywhere." He indicated the alchemy shop behind them with his thumb. "I could go through there if I wanted to, and come out in Séadna Tobín's shop. It wouldn't be a particularly smart idea, but I could do it."

"How?"

"I don't know," said Aengus. "It comes naturally to us. How do you breathe?"

"Do you go through a lot, then?"

"Not in the normal course of events. When the sun was where it ought to be, we only went through now and then for a bit of craic. Or when we had to."

J.J. thought about it. "So the time skin must be everywhere?"

"It is," said Aengus. "There are a few places where it had to be closed off, but it's almost everywhere."

"So something must have broken it," said J.J.

"It looks like it," said Aengus, "but I don't see how it can have. You've seen the way it operates. During the war a group of your lads decided to have a go at destroying it. I watched them hacking at it with swords and axes. They might as well have been trying to cut a hole in the sea."

"But there's a hole in it now," said J.J. "Has there ever been a leak before?"

"We never had a 'before' before," said Aengus. "There are other kinds of leaks, of course. But they're harmless."

"What other kinds of leaks?" said J.J.

"Well, the music, for one. That leaks through all over the place."

"Could the time be coming with it?"

"It never has," said Aengus. "I can't see what would make it start doing it now."

"Maybe we should check it out all the same," said J.J.

"If you like," said Aengus. "Winkles is as good a place as any."

They stood up and began to walk back down the street. Bran, who had been lying down beside J.J. while they talked, heaved herself up and followed them.

When they got to the square, Aengus handed his

fiddle case to J.J. "Take this and go on down there. I'll borrow another one and catch up with you."

"We're not going to play tunes," said J.J. "Lesson number two of how to worry. No tunes."

"And how do you expect to check out a music leak without music?" said Aengus.

J.J. conceded the point and took the fiddle. When Aengus crossed the road toward Drowsy Maggie's house, Bran didn't follow him. She stayed with J.J. and followed him, step by painful step, along the street toward Winkles.

The inside of the pub was so dim that J.J. had to stand in the doorway until his eyes adjusted. When they did, he saw that Jennie and Marcus were already there, sitting in the corner between the door and the fireplace. Devaney was there as well, up at the bar.

"Welcome back," he said to J.J.

"Sit down here," said Jennie. "We were thinking of having a tune."

It was the first building in Tír na n'Óg that J.J. had gone into, and the inside of it appeared even more organic than the outside. The tables and chairs were constructed, quite haphazardly, from whole branches, some of which still had leaves attached to them.

"Did you see herself around anywhere?" said Devaney.

"Who?"

"His goat," said Marcus. "Can't have much of a tune without her."

J.J. shook his head and sat on a stool, surprised to find that it felt much more substantial than it looked. It was so substantial, in fact, that when he tried to shuffle it closer to the table it wouldn't budge an inch. He looked down between his feet and saw that its legs, and those of the table as well, disappeared into the packed earth of the floor. All the furniture, including the bar itself, was still growing.

Devaney got down from his bar stool and went to the door. "I'll go and have a look for her," he said, and went out.

"If I'm not mistaken," said Marcus, "that fiddle case belongs to Aengus Óg."

"Aengus Óg?" said J.J. "Is that who he is?"

"Who else would he be?" said Jennie.

The others, including the maid behind the bar, laughed.

"But I thought Aengus Óg was a god," said J.J.

"Don't let him hear you say that," said Marcus. "He has a high enough opinion of himself as it is."

"He's not, then?" said J.J.

"No more than any of us," said Jennie.

"If it's gods you're looking for, you've come to the wrong place," said Marcus.

The barmaid came over with a wineglass filled with amber fluid for Jennie and something in a yellow bottle, which she put down in front of Marcus.

"Anything for J.J.?" said Marcus.

"What does J.J. want?" said the barmaid.

"Coke?" said J.J.

The girl hunted through the rows of bottles behind the bar and lifted one down. It was the old-fashioned, chunky kind of bottle and J.J. wondered how long it had been there. But when it opened with a satisfying gasp of fizz, he remembered that, until a few hours ago, there had been no time at all in Tír na n'Óg.

Something in the back of his mind needled at him and made him feel uneasy. Something to do with the bottle and its age, and its freshness. But Jennie laughed and pointed to the door, and what he saw there made him forget whatever it was that had been bothering him.

The goat was standing in the doorway, looking in at them.

"She likes the music really," said Marcus. "But winding up Devaney is even more craic."

"Should we catch her?" said J.J.

"Na," said Marcus. "Don't want to spoil Devaney's fun."

The barmaid came over with the Coke.

"How much?" said J.J., before he remembered that they didn't use money.

"No charge for musicians," said the girl.

Since there was no one in the place apart from musicians, J.J. wondered if Aengus might not be the only person in Tír na n'Óg who hadn't quite grasped the concept of profit.

"What's in the yellow bottle?" said J.J.

"I don't know," said Marcus, "but it does the trick. Do you know that tune? 'The Yellow Bottle'?"

"I know a tune called 'The Yellow Wattle,' " said J.J.

"That's the one," said Marcus. "Sometimes the names get mixed up on the way through to your side."

"Sometimes they don't get through at all," said Jennie. "That's why there are so many tunes that have no names, or that get called after the person who first plays them."

"Or the people who think they wrote them," said Marcus.

Aengus arrived with the borrowed fiddle. He clapped his hands and rubbed them together vigorously. "The yellow bottle looks like the order of the day," he said breezily.

"Hold on a minute," said J.J. "How to worry, rule number three. No alcohol."

A flash of anger blazed in Aengus's clear green eyes. J.J.'s spirits dropped into his boots, and for an instant he was afraid of how Aengus might react. But he was saved by a commotion in the street outside; a sudden burst of bleats and roars, followed by a hollow, knocking sound. Then Devaney came in through the door with the bodhrán.

Everyone let out a cheer. Devaney joined the group in the corner, and Aengus opened Maggie's fiddle case. He showed no more signs of being annoyed with J.J.

"Let's see about finding this leak then, shall we?" he said.

THE YELLOW WATTLE

Trad

There were no musicians playing that night in Winkles, nor in Green's nor the Auld Plaid Shawl, nor in any of the other pubs in Kinvara. J.J. Liddy was young, but he was one of their number nonetheless. As long as he was missing, there would be no live music heard in their town.

Anne Korff received a visit from Sergeant Early on Tuesday evening. She told him her story, showed him the punctured bike tire, and expressed enormous regret at not having insisted that J.J. take a lift with her. Sergeant Early assured her that she had done nothing wrong and was adamant that she shouldn't blame herself.

But J.J.'s parents, their neighbors, and half the local

community were out walking the roads and scouring the coastline, and Anne Korff did blame herself. She had been wrong to send the boy on such a hopeless errand. It was high time she fetched him back.

It was difficult to worry while the fairy music was playing, even for J.J., who was a master of the art. As soon as the tunes started flowing, he forgot all about leaks, musical or otherwise, and settled in to enjoy himself.

Gradually the pub filled up. Some danced, some listened and watched, some joined in with hilarious recitations or with songs so sorrowful that there was not a dry eye in the place when they reached their end.

Aengus, under loud and frequent protest, drank nothing but water throughout the session. In his honor the musicians played "The Teetotaller's Reel" on three different occasions, and they might have played it again had Aengus not become edgy and threatened to turn them all into "something nocturnal and slimy."

J.J. learned more in that session than he would have believed possible. At least half the tunes that were played he had never heard before, and he had to concentrate hard to pick up their gist. Sometimes, when he heard one he particularly liked, he asked Aengus or one of the others to go over some of the trickier lines with him. He didn't expect to have them perfectly, or anything like it, but he knew that he would be able to play along with them if they came up again in sessions. Their names he forgot as soon as he had heard them.

And that wasn't all that he learned. By the time he had joined in a few sets of tunes he was, Aengus remarked encouragingly, playing like a native. The fairy rhythms and their subtle intonations seemed to be in his blood. He had never felt more at ease with a fiddle beneath his chin. It was as though he had been practicing for this all his life.

But the one thing that J.J. did not encounter that afternoon was a music leak. The others described to him how it happened; how other instruments could be heard, playing faintly in the gap between the tunes and how, if the leak was strong enough, the two groups of musicians, one in each world, could join in each other's tunes and end up with a mighty session. J.J. would have loved to hear it, but it didn't happen. No matter how hard he listened, he could hear no notes, corresponding or otherwise, leaking through the time skin.

"It's very unusual," Marcus remarked. "Especially in here. It's a very leaky place."

"The leakiest," said Jennie.

Aengus went out to take a stroll and see if there was anything coming through in any of the other pubs. In the street he ran into Anne Korff, who was outside the door talking to Bran.

"How's life, Lucy?" he said.

Anne laughed. "To tell you the truth," she said, "it could be better."

"I'm glad to hear it," said Aengus. "Are you going in for a pint?"

"No. I'm just going to put my head round the door. I'm looking for someone."

"Oh? Anyone I know?"

"A young man from our side. J.J. Liddy. I did a very stupid thing. He wanted to buy some time, and I sent him here to see what he could find out. Now his poor mother and father are going demented, searching for him everywhere."

"The poor things," said Aengus. "But you're in luck. He hasn't gone far."

"No? You have seen him?"

"Yes," said Aengus. "He tried to give me ten euro

for our time. I told him if he could find the leak he could have it for nothing. So he went off looking for it."

"Which way did he go?"

Aengus pointed to the Galway road, which ran out of the village past the castle. "He was heading for the gravel walks when I last saw him."

"I'll find him out there then," said Anne. "Thank you, Aengus."

"No bother." Aengus watched Anne until she had disappeared down the main street of the village, then he continued on his way.

It seemed to J.J. that they played for hours, but since his watch wasn't working, or was working to some harebrained scheme of its own, he had no way of telling. Whenever anyone came in or went out, the doorway filled with brilliant sunlight. There was, he kept reminding himself, plenty of time.

Aengus came and went two or three times during the course of the session, and at one stage J.J. suspected that he was nipping over to Keogh's or down to Tully's for a quick drink of something stronger. But if he was, he showed no signs of it, and his playing, which was an education in itself to J.J., didn't show any ill effects following his absences.

It was Aengus who, eventually, announced the end of the session by putting the borrowed fiddle back in its case. J.J. followed suit.

"You may as well finish up your drink," he said. "I'll pop this fiddle back in to Maggie and come back for you. Then we can have a think about what to do next."

THE GRAVEL WALKS

Trad

J.J. sat down on the footpath beside Bran and leaned against the wall. There was, he noticed, a small puddle of blood beside the damaged leg. Bran squirmed closer and rested her head in his lap. She made no sound, but she fidgeted constantly, finding no comfort. Occasionally a deep shudder ran through her whole body. J.J. scratched her ears and tried not to look at the horrible injury.

The warmth of the day made him drowsy. He surrendered to the feeling and allowed his heavy eyelids to close. The brightness of the sun turned his vision red inside them.

Something was wrong.

He opened his eyes again. Throughout the whole of that long session in the pub the sun had scarcely moved in the sky. Instinctively he looked at his watch. Six ten. He put it to his ear. Tick . . . silence . . . tick.

There was, he finally realized, nothing at all wrong with the watch. He had arrived in Tír na n'Óg at the beginning of time. It had not established itself here yet; had barely disturbed the pristine stillness of eternity. He couldn't hope to fully understand what was happening, but he was beginning to get an inkling of how it might work, like a force that was slowly gathering momentum. His best guess was that Tír na n'Óg was only receiving a tiny trickle of time. But even this slow leak was far more than his own world could afford to lose.

It meant, at least, that he would probably be home in time for the céilí. Or did it? The uneasy feeling returned. Was that right? Was it only six ten at home? Or was time passing faster there? Another penny was teetering, about to drop, but J.J. was distracted by the sudden appearance of the goat. She sprang out through the door, gave J.J. a look of utter disdain, and bounded off toward the main street.

Bran sighed and turned to lick her wound. J.J. looked away. Maggie came out of her door with her fiddle case. She waved to him and walked down toward the quay. The goat looked up and down the street, then turned to follow her. There were other people drifting down that way as well, and J.J. wondered if there was going to be another dance. He noticed that one or two of them glanced up at the sky as they went, but other than that he saw no signs of anxiety in the village. How could they be thinking about dancing? Why was everyone not out searching for the leak? Perhaps, whatever Aengus and the other musicians had said, it just wasn't bad enough here to be worth worrying about. Maybe they didn't realize how bad things were on the other side? Or didn't care?

In his imagination he saw a bleak picture: the planet spinning like a tennis ball, its occupants chasing around frantically as they tried to fit their lives into their ever-diminishing time spans. The trouble was, how would they know where to start looking? Even if you were standing right on top of the leak, how would you know? You couldn't see time, or hear it, or smell it.

Devaney and the others strolled out of the pub.

"Coming down to the quay?" asked Jennie.

"Don't you think it would be better to look for the leak?" J.J. asked her.

They all looked up at the sky, then at one another, then back at J.J.

"Ah, here's Aengus," said Marcus, sounding enormously relieved.

He had appeared round the corner of the street and was coming toward them. The others greeted him briefly, then went on their way to the dance.

"You sure you don't want to join them?" said Aengus.

"Lesson number four," said J.J. "No dancing."

Aengus closed his eyes, and J.J. wondered if he might be hiding another of those angry moments. But when he opened them again, he was as chirpy as ever. "So what's the plan?" he said.

"I don't know," said J.J. "I was hoping you might have one."

"Not really," said Aengus. He thought for a moment, then went on, "You're a farm lad, aren't you?"

"You could say that," said J.J.

"You must have spent a bit of time up in the hills and out on the land."

"I have. Why?"

"Well, did you never come across any kind of a leak?"

"I don't think so," said J.J. "I never heard music, anyway."

"Nothing else?" said Aengus. "You never saw anything that shouldn't be there or heard people talking?"

"No," said J.J. But Aengus was getting out his tobacco, and it reminded him of something that had happened when he'd been up in the hazel woods above the farm, searching for a lost goat. "I smelled smoke once, though. Tobacco smoke. And there was no one there."

"That's exactly the kind of thing we're looking for," said Aengus. "Where was it?"

J.J. told him.

"That's where we'll go, so," said Aengus.

FREE AND EASY

Trad

9

It was a long walk up to Eagle's Rock, at the foot of which lay the woods where J.J., in his own world, had smelled tobacco smoke. J.J. was dreading it, particularly when he realized that Bran, despite the best efforts of Aengus to stop her, was determined to go with them. But once they got out onto the road that cut across the plain below the mountains, J.J. forgot about the journey. The sun was warm and bright and the lush, green farmlands were so unspoiled that it made J.J. aware, for the first time, of how drab and tired his own world was becoming. If it wasn't for the socks, it would have been perfect. There hadn't been many in the village, but on this road there seemed to be even more than there had been on his way in from Doorus. He wanted to ask Aengus about them, but there were other things that seemed more important.

"I still don't get the bit about immortality," he said. "If you live forever, then you must be immortal."

"No," said Aengus. "If we were in your world now and a bus came flying round that corner, it could kill me just as easily as it could kill you." He shuddered. "I hate buses," he said.

"Me, too," said J.J. "Especially these days. They're always late."

"Doesn't surprise me," said Aengus. "But there's a good enough reason for the immortality misunderstanding. We don't go across as much as we used to. At least we didn't"—he waved both arms in the air—"until all this. But there was a period in your history when we used to come and go more freely. Thing is, you'd meet someone over there and come home again, and then when you went over and bumped into them again thirty or forty years might have passed in your world."

The information made J.J. uneasy again, but he was too curious about too many things to pay the feeling any attention. "I thought you weren't allowed to go there," he said. "I thought you had an agreement."

"We cheated," said Aengus. "We had to."

"Why?"

"Because of our children. If we wanted to repro-
duce ourselves, and most people do, you know, we had
to use your world to do it." Aengus was having difficulty keeping his pipe lit, and he stopped to puff at it
for a minute, then went on. "We love this world.
Anyone who sees it does. But it has its drawbacks. Life
without time is perfect when you get to my age, but it's
not much use if you want to do a bit of growing up."

"I see what you mean," said J.J. "If there's no time,
you never get any older."

"Spot on," said Aengus. "Pregnancies need time
and so do births, but most of all, babies need time to
grow up."

"So you have to go over there to live when you have
children?"

"Not exactly," said Aengus. "We could, technically,
but who wants to get fifteen or twenty years older if
they don't have to?"

"How do you do it then?" said J.J.

"Did you ever hear of changelings?"

J.J. nodded. The word gave him the creeps.

"What did you hear about them?" said Aengus.

"That the f— that the fairies used to take someone's baby and leave one of their own in its place."

"You didn't think it was true, did you?" said Aengus.

"Of course not," said J.J. In his primary school they had done a huge project, gathering together folklore from the old people in the village and the surrounding farms. They had collected dozens of fairy stories, several of them about changelings. It had never occurred to him that there could be anything other than imagination behind them. He still couldn't believe it. That word "fairies" was getting in the way.

"Well, it is," said Aengus. "It's not so easy these days, of course, what with hospital births and burglar alarms and baby monitors and all that malarkey. But we still get the odd few across."

"Don't they look different?" said J.J. "In the stories I heard the babies were all ugly little creatures."

"Everybody thinks their own baby is beautiful and everyone else's is ugly," said Aengus. "But what can people do, when it comes down to it? Who's going to believe them if they kick up about it? And a baby's a baby when all's said and done. They just have to get on with it."

J.J. hesitated before he asked the next question, afraid to hear what the answer might be. "What do you do with the babies that you take away?"

"That's not so hard," said Aengus. "We put them in a basket, take them a few counties away, and leave them on someone's doorstep."

"But that doesn't make sense," said J.J. "Why don't you save all the hassle and just leave your own babies on doorsteps?"

"We're fussy, that's why. We choose our foster parents carefully. We don't want to leave our children with just anyone, you know."

"But you don't care about other people's children," said J.J. spitefully.

"Caring is another of those things like worrying," said Aengus. "We're useless at it. We just don't get enough practice."

But he seemed to care about Bran, judging by the way he stopped every hundred meters or so to let her catch up. He did it again now, and while they were waiting, he began to examine a dark green sock that was hanging, among others, on a nearby bush. "That's not a bad one," he said, taking it down and trying it against the ones he was wearing. They were, J.J. couldn't help noticing, not just odd, but different colors.

"What do you think?" said Aengus.

"It doesn't go with either of them," said J.J. "What

is the story with all these socks, anyway?"

"Ah," said Aengus, putting the sock back on the bush and trying out another one. "That's another leak. The sock leak."

J.J. laughed incredulously. "A sock leak?!"

"What did you think?" said Aengus irritably. "That we went over and stole all these socks from you people and scattered them all over the place?"

"Well, no," said J.J. "But—"

"It's the washing machines that cause it," said Aengus. "Or maybe the dryers. No one knows why."

J.J. remembered the pillowcase in the hot press at home, stuffed to bursting with odd socks. Some of them had been waiting for years to be reunited with their lost partners. Helen had tried to throw them all out once, but Ciaran hadn't let her. He said that if she did, the others were sure to turn up again immediately. "Sod's law," he called it.

"Why do you just leave them there?" said J.J.

"Who's going to pick them up?" said Aengus. "Apart from when they feel like a change of socks?" He changed one of his own, as if to demonstrate, hopping on one foot as he did it. "Besides," he went on, "they're useful markers for us."

"Markers for what?" said J.J.

"There's so many new houses going up on your side that we can't keep track of them. There's a danger that one of us could go over and find ourselves in the middle of someone's kitchen. Or worse. But the socks tell us where the new houses are. We don't mind them really."

Bran had caught up and plonked herself down in the road, but she had to get straight up again as Aengus and J.J. moved off. Before long they came to where the Moy Road crossed the New Line and Aengus paused there for a while, looking around and listening.

"What are you looking for?" J.J. asked him.

"Nothing in particular," said Aengus. "But crossroads are leaky places. You never know what you might find."

"Is that why we used to have dances at the crossroads?" said J.J.

"It is," said Aengus. "You're catching on at last."

He led the way across the New Line and up the mountain road that led to Colman's church and Eagle's Rock. J.J.'s house was nearby, over to the right. The drive opened off the New Line farther down, but it would be easy for them to get to it across country from where they were, and it wouldn't take long. He would have liked to see what it looked like in this world, but when he proposed the idea Aengus shook his head.

"Maybe we can go back down that way," he said. "I don't want to waste time."

"Well, that's progress," said J.J. "Maybe it's you who should be giving me the worrying lessons."

Ahead of them the road ran through thickets of hazel, which seemed, from the sounds of it, to be full of woodpeckers.

"We don't get many of them on our side," said J.J.

"Many what?" said Aengus.

"Woodpeckers," said J.J.

"Is there a woodpecker?" said Aengus.

"Can't you hear them?" said J.J.

"What I'm hearing isn't woodpeckers," said Aengus. He took the fiddle case from his shoulder and handed it to J.J. "Will you hold on to this for a while? I have a bit of business to take care of."

"What kind of business?" said J.J.

"Just business," said Aengus, but his eyes warned J.J. not to ask any more about it. "Stay on the road now, you hear me? Don't go into the woods whatever else you do."

"Why not?"

"Leprechauns," said Aengus. "The place is thick with them."

"Leprechauns?" said J.J., coming to the realization that the sounds he was hearing might not, after all, be woodpeckers. "What would they do to me?"

"Oh, I don't know," said Aengus irritably. "Make shoes at you or something. Just keep to the road, all right? When you see the pigeon on the gate, stop and wait for me there."

"How do you know there'll be a pigeon on the gate?" said J.J.

"Because there . . ." Aengus hesitated. "Good point. Everything's different now, isn't it? Wait at the oak tree then. I don't suppose that will have gone anywhere."

He disappeared among the trees. J.J. was tempted to follow and find out for himself about leprechauns, but now that he thought about it there was something sinister about those sharp little machine-gun bursts of hammering. And if he got into some kind of trouble there would be no chance of finding the time leak. It would be better to play safe.

He walked slowly so that Bran, who was making heavy weather of the hill, could stay with him. If what Aengus had told him about the changelings was true, and he had to admit that it made perfect sense, did that mean that the other old stories were true as well? Did the fairies dance in the ring forts at night? Did people hear leaks there, and go to sleep, and wake up to find that seven years had passed? Did Aengus and the others visit bad luck on people who took stones from the forts, or who built their houses on the paths they used, or who failed to leave out milk for them when they were used to getting it?

Milk? J.J. couldn't imagine Aengus getting shirty about a glass of milk. He looked down at Bran, still battling on behind him. If she was who Aengus said she was, did that mean that Fionn was here as well? Were the Fianna walking around in these gray hills with their broadswords and their beards? J.J. had read all those old stories in primary school, but he couldn't remember any of them now, apart from his favorite one, about Diarmuid and Gráinne. There were sites scattered all over the country that were supposed to have been beds where the two lovers had lain together. Was there a chance that they could still be out there somewhere, condemned to spend eternity fleeing the wrath of Fionn?

PIGEON ON THE GATE

Trad

The case of the missing teenager had come to a standstill. Extensive inquiries and searches had turned up nothing. Now, to add to the disquiet in the locality, Anne Korff seemed to have disappeared as well. The police, after looking into the matter, refused to make any connection between the two incidents. Anne Korff's house was locked up from the outside. It was undisturbed. Wherever she had gone, she had taken her dog with her. Unlike J.J. Liddy, she was an adult, and if she chose to go away without telling her friends, that was her concern. There was no evidence of a crime, and there was no reason to investigate.

The villagers were of a different opinion. They kept their doors locked at all times, and few of them ventured out alone at night. The pubs were quiet and closed on time. The local teenagers were subdued and had no inclination to prowl the streets or even to drink scrumpy around the back of the primary school. There was nothing whatsoever for a policeman to do in the village, but it was imperative that one should be seen there. The new guy was given the job.

Larry O'Dwyer walked slowly but, he hoped, authoritatively, up and down the main street of Kinvara. Everyone who passed stopped to ask him for the latest news and to give him their theory on the missing people. This, Larry was almost certain, was not why he had become a policeman, but he succeeded in remaining courteous and respectful. Only one person tried his patience, and that was Thomas O'Neill.

He began by asking the usual questions and continued on to give Larry an account of one of the widely accepted theories. But as he spoke he looked at him rather too closely for comfort.

"I know you," he said, when Larry had congratulated him on the pertinence of his theory and assured him that he and his colleagues would bear it in mind. "It's coming to me now."

Larry hoped that it wasn't. He could really do without the kind of trouble that a man of Thomas's age and status could create for him. Spotting Phil

Daly on the other side of the road, he made rapid excuses and crossed over to talk to him.

Phil asked the usual questions, but if he had a theory he kept it to himself. "I was looking for you last week," he said. "I wanted to invite you to a céilí."

"Oh," said Larry. "I wish you'd found me."

"Yeah," said Phil ruefully. "It was good. But it was at the Liddy house. I don't suppose there'll be another one now. Not for a good while, anyway."

"You never know," said Larry. "I'd say the lad could still turn up."

The rest of the day sped past, despite the lack of activity. The only noteworthy thing that happened was the sudden appearance, from the quiet street that ran down past the community center, of a white donkey. Nobody knew who owned it or where it had come from. Very few people kept donkeys anymore.

It shouldn't really have been police business, but since Larry was in the village anyway and had nothing much else to do, he got drawn into the debate about what should be done with it. It was a placid creature and a source of great amusement to the school-children, but it was a nuisance to traffic and couldn't be allowed to stay there. Sergeant Early blew a minor fuse when Larry radioed him for advice, and for a while Larry was at a loss to know what to do. He stood outside Fallon's with his arm round the donkey's neck until the word got around and one of the local horse owners came and agreed to take charge of it until someone came to claim it.

THE WHITE DONKEY

Kate Thompson

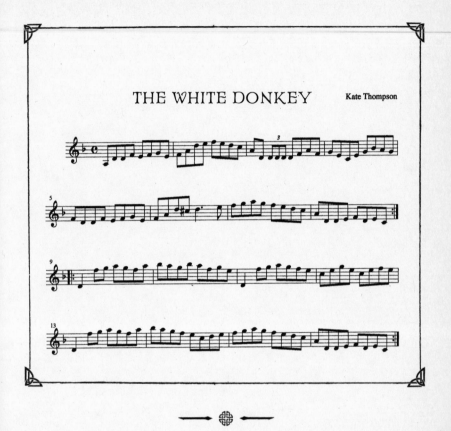

There was, after all, a pigeon on the gate. While he was waiting for Aengus, J.J. took out the fiddle and ran the bow over the strings to see what he could come up with. The notion still lingered in his mind that if he could only remember "Dowd's Number Nine" the whole time situation might miraculously resolve itself. When he failed, he had a go at remembering some of the tunes he had played with the others in Winkles that evening, and when he came to a dead end with those, he played "The Pigeon on the Gate."

"That's the wrong 'Pigeon on the Gate,'" said Aengus, emerging from the hazel.

J.J. looked at the bird. Aengus took the fiddle and played a different tune. It was in the same key and the first few notes were the same, but it was a mellower, more haunting tune. J.J. hadn't heard it before, but he had yet another version. He took the fiddle back. "Where's this pigeon then?" he asked, and played it.

Aengus shrugged. "Could be anywhere."

J.J. played "The Bird in the Bush." Aengus laughed and danced a few lively steps on the road. J.J. was enjoying himself, but Aengus took the fiddle back and put it away. "You're a poor teacher," he said. "Very slack for a ploddy."

"A what?"

"A ploddy," said Aengus. "You have a name for us. Did you think we wouldn't have one for you?"

"But . . . ploddy?"

"Is it any worse than fairy?" said Aengus. He slung the fiddle over his shoulder again and they walked on up the road. There was something odd about him, and it was a while before J.J. realized what it was.

"You changed your shirt," he said.

Aengus looked down at himself as though he wasn't sure what he was wearing. "Oh, yes," he said. "I didn't mention that, did I?"

"Mention what?"

"The leprechaun laundry. That was my business with them. They wash clothes."

J.J. found it unlikely, but who was he to argue? "They wash your shirts," he said, "and you pay them with gold?"

"Well," said Aengus, "that's what they'll be hoping, yes."

Behind them the frantic hammering faded into the distance and died away. When they stopped again to wait for Bran, J.J.'s thoughts returned to the changelings.

"Do you go back for them?" he asked Aengus. "Your children?"

"No, no," said Aengus. "We just forget about them. They come back when they're ready."

"What, you mean they just turn up?"

"They do. They're usually about your age when they get here, give or take a year or two."

"But how do they get through?" said J.J. "And how do they even know they're . . ." He hesitated, then decided that, since Aengus had called him a ploddy, there were no holds barred. "How do they know they're fairies?"

They had reached the highest point on the road and Aengus turned in at a gap in the hedge. There was a path, as there was in J.J.'s world, which led toward the hazel woods at the bottom of Eagle's Rock.

"You know about cuckoos, I suppose," said Aengus.

"A bit," said J.J. "I know they lay their eggs in other birds' nests."

"They do," said Aengus. "And then they head straight back home to Africa. The chicks hatch out in Ireland, grow up in Ireland, learn to fly in Ireland, and then, when they're ready, they head off for Africa as well."

"Really?" said J.J. "But how do they know how to get to Africa?"

"The same way our children know how to get here," said Aengus.

"It must be some sort of instinct," said J.J.

"It might be," said Aengus, "though I suspect that word 'instinct' might be used by your scientists to explain any kind of animal behavior that they don't understand. Did you know that cuckoos were originally from here?"

"No," said J.J., though now that he was thinking about it he remembered that he'd heard them referred to as "fairy birds."

Aengus paused to lift Bran into his arms. They were crossing some awkward, stony ground and she was having difficulty. "Same principle, you see?" he said. "They used to lay their eggs in ploddyland and come home. Their chicks borrowed some of your time to grow up, then followed their parents back here."

"Then why don't they still do it?" asked J.J.

"Airplanes," said Aengus, putting Bran carefully back onto her three feet.

"What about airplanes?" said J.J.

Aengus looked up. "Do you see any?"

J.J. scanned the sky. "No."

"There aren't any, that's why. We had to close the sky gates when your crowd learned to fly. It was way too dangerous."

"There were sky gates?"

"All over the place," said Aengus. "For the cuckoos. But we couldn't have planeloads of ploddies landing in on top of us, could we? Besides, they're dreadful, noisy, smelly things, the same airplanes. Sad, but we had to say good-bye to the cuckoos."

They walked on along the stony path. It ran through a big rocky meadow; windswept and bleak in J.J.'s world but serene here, and littered with clover and cranesbill. There were no socks to be seen anywhere.

"How did you do it?" asked J.J. "Close the sky gates?"

"I don't know," said Aengus. "My dad takes care of

all that stuff. He had to close the sea gates as well when you started building submarines. The merrows are all stuck here now."

"What if one of them was left open?" said J.J. "By mistake, I mean. Couldn't the time be coming through there?"

"It wouldn't follow," said Aengus. "The time skin is the same there as it is down here. One of them did get left open for a while, actually. Dad just forgot about it. Quite a few planes came through before he copped on to it. The ploddies called it the Bermuda Triangle."

"But that's miles away," said J.J. "How could the planes get into Tír na n'Óg?"

"Our world is the same size as yours, J.J. Same seas, same continents, same everything except time."

J.J. sat down on a slab of rock. "That's crazy," he said. "That means the leak could be anywhere. Anywhere in the whole world!"

There was no answer. J.J. turned to where Aengus had been standing. Bran was lying in the grass, licking her injured leg, but Aengus was nowhere to be seen.

THE CUCKOO'S NEST

Trad

"Aengus?" he called.

"What?" Aengus was standing right behind him, exactly where he had expected him to be when he turned around. But he hadn't been there last time he looked, he was certain of it.

"I didn't see you there," said J.J. "My eyes must be playing tricks on me."

"How odd," said Aengus. "You'd never get to the bottom of what goes on in a ploddy mind."

He walked on across the hillside, and J.J. followed. Ahead of them Eagle's Rock rose up, a sheer cliff climbing out of the scrubby woods that ran along its base. There was no breeze, and the silence was absolute until a spine-tingling cry rang out from the crag. Bran's hackles stood up and she growled.

It was the first sound that J.J. had heard her make.

"What was that?" he asked Aengus.

"It wasn't a leprechaun, anyway," said Aengus. "They don't come up this high."

They went on again. Bran's hackles stayed raised, but there was no more sound from the rock. At the edge of the wood, where the little path ran in toward Colman's cave, Aengus turned to J.J.

"Where was it you smelled the tobacco smoke?"

J.J. knew those woods well in his own world. There had been a time when he visited them a lot, just to breathe the cool air and enjoy the undisturbed mystery of the place. But here they gave him the creeps. He wasn't at all sure he wanted to go in.

"About halfway along, I think," he said. "But I might not have smelled anything, now I come to think of it. I could have imagined it."

"That's what ploddies always say about leaks," said Aengus. "Come on."

He led the way in among the trees. The sun's light slanted through the branches, covering the mossy floor with patchy shadows. Bran was still on edge and J.J. sensed that, despite his nonchalant air, Aengus was as well. As they passed a young blackthorn, a little flock of wrens ticked and whirred at them like a bush-full of tiny clocks. Other than that there was no sound in the woods, apart from their own careful footsteps. "Around here?" said Aengus after a while.

"A bit farther on, I think," J.J. whispered. "It's hard to tell."

After another hundred meters he pulled at Aengus's elbow. "About here, I think."

"Right." Aengus stopped and looked all around. "I'm going to have to go through for a while."

"Go through?" said J.J.

"I won't be gone long, but I can't check out the wall without going through it." He handed J.J. the fiddle. "You'll be safe enough here with Bran."

"Okay," said J.J.

"Don't talk to any goats, all right?"

"Goats?" said J.J., but Aengus was already gone, slipping lightly away between the straight stalks of the hazel and then . . .

Where?

J.J. wished that Bran wasn't so nervous. She was lying down again, but not in the usual way. She wasn't resting. Her ears were pricked, and she was staring fixedly in the direction of the crag, as though expecting something to appear at any moment. J.J. sat on a mossy rock. It was damp, despite the dryness of the day, but he didn't get up again. He was developing the most awful feeling that he was being watched.

He put the fiddle case down on the ground, but he wasn't inclined to open it. He felt far too exposed. The damp was soaking into his jeans, but still he stayed where he was.

"Good girl, Bran," he said quietly, as much to mask the silence as anything. In response, she growled again, a low rumble from deep in her chest. J.J. broke out in goose bumps. Bran was staring through the trees. There was something there.

J.J. let out a long-held breath. "It's only a goat, Bran," he said. He was used to the wild goats up here on the mountainside. They were a menace to the farmers, but J.J. had a grudging respect for them all the same. They came and went as they pleased, caring nothing for walls or fences, or carefully preserved meadows. On more than one occasion Helen and Ciaran had lost good milkers to the herds that roamed up here, and whenever J.J. saw the wild goats, he thought of them and wondered what their lives must be like away from the comforts of the farmyard, off with the raggle-taggle gypsies.

But were goats here the same? This one certainly

wasn't behaving like the ones he had encountered here before. They usually kept out of sight, and if he took them by surprise, as occasionally happened, they lost no time in getting out of his way. But this goat was coming toward him. And it was, he now realized, the biggest one he had ever seen.

Bran's reaction was not inspiring him with confidence. She was clearly terrified of the goat, alternately attempting to protect J.J. with hysterical growling and taking refuge behind him. Ignoring her completely, the huge goat kept coming.

J.J. stood up. The goat stopped about twenty meters away. It had a jaunty, almost humorous expression, as though it might be on for a bit of craic. J.J. hoped that it wouldn't be at his expense. He had seen more goat horns than most people, but he had never seen a pair of horns that size. They were as thick and as long as his arms, and an awful lot more dangerous.

He would have felt a lot safer behind a large rock or a tree trunk, but he couldn't move; couldn't even look around to see where he would run if it turned out that he had to. The goat's yellow eyes, their narrow, vertical pupils, had him mesmerized. There was a sharp, dangerous intelligence in them. They were full of fun and full of disaster. Bran had given up the battle with her pride and was cringing behind J.J.'s back.

"I know you," said a rich, dark voice. J.J. couldn't tell whether it came from the air around him or from inside his head. "I've seen you in here before."

J.J. was about to reply when Aengus's words came back to him. "Don't talk to any goats."

"Not here, perhaps," said the goat. "Over on the other side, was it?"

Still J.J. said nothing. The goat's expression didn't change, but there was a smile in its voice. "Aengus Óg has been filling your head with nonsense, I see. Well. That's the way with the sidhe."

J.J. had almost forgotten the old word for the fairies. It could mean a hill, or the people of the hill. It carried very different connotations.

"Tricky folk," said the disembodied voice of the goat. "Not to be trusted. Spun you some yarn about a time leak, has he?"

J.J. held his tongue, but it wasn't easy. The goat frightened him, but it didn't appear to want to harm him.

"Slipped over beyond, hasn't he?" the voice continued. "Off flirting with some young one, I'd be willing to bet. A bit of a lad, your Aengus Óg. The wild Irishman, with his fiddle and his charm and his little bit of magic."

J.J. was feeling sleepy. He wanted to defend Aengus; he didn't want to hear any more malicious talk, but there was something about the deep, mellow tones in that voice that made him want to listen.

"Tired?" said the goat. "Awful warm in here, isn't it?"

J.J.'s mind drifted. The green moss, smelling of water, the dappled shadows, the warm sun, the warm voice; they were the things of dreams. His eyelids closed. The dream sounds and smells grew deeper and stronger. But something moved between him and the sun. His eyelids and his skin sensed the shadow.

With a struggle he opened his eyes. The thing that stood in front of him was not a goat. It had horns, cloven feet, but it was towering on two legs; tall as the trees, looming over him.

"Aengus!" he yelled at the top of his voice. Bran found her courage and was at his side, snapping and barking. The thing shrank, became a goat again, stood looking out at them, as quietly confident as ever.

"Do you know what I am?" said the voice.

J.J. almost answered, stopped himself just in time. He was shaking from head to foot.

"Do you know who we are, who walk between the worlds and haunt the wild places of the earth?"

J.J. felt his energy begin to flag again. He was being drawn in by the voice.

"Do you want to know the real magic that is at work in the world?"

J.J. put his hands over his eyes and his ears. He hummed to himself there in the shady woods, and the tune that he hummed was the one his mother had taught him less than twenty-four hours ago.

Something gripped his wrist. He clenched his teeth and resisted with all his might, keeping his eyes and ears closed.

"J.J.!" He heard his name close to his ear and, carefully, peeped out between his fingers. It was Aengus.

THE WILD IRISHMAN

Trad

Anne Korff, with Lottie at her heels, walked back into the village. J.J. Liddy had not been on the gravel walks or anywhere in their vicinity, and Anne was beginning to suspect that he never had been. She berated herself. She ought to have known better than to trust anything Aengus Óg told her. This was by no means the first time he had sent her on a wild goose chase. She remembered the occasion when he had offered to indulge her passion for sailing by letting her take his sleek little boat, the *Salamanca*, for a sail in the bay. He had whistled up a perfect offshore breeze, which had sent her speeding out past Augnish and around the mouth of the bay. But no sooner had she gone about to begin the return trip than he turned off the wind and dropped an enormous cloud on the surface of the water.

The boats of the sidhe have no engines. It happened before the passage of time was appreciable in Tír na n'Óg, but even so Anne Korff had learned far more than she wanted to know about the insides of clouds.

In the village, between dances, Anne asked Drowsy Maggie if she had seen J.J. Maggie could not tell her where he was now, but she did tell her where he had been when Anne had bumped into Aengus outside Winkles. She stood with Lottie on the harbor wall and looked out to sea. There was no sense at all in tearing off to look for them again; there were far too many places where they might be. She knew the dangers of lingering too long in the land of eternal youth, but she knew, as well, that everything was changing. If things carried on as they were, she might never get a chance to see it in the same way again. Another dance or two would not hurt.

When the musicians started up again, she stepped into the crowd; felt the familiar lightness in her feet and in her heart as all her concerns slipped away. As long as J.J. remembered what she had told him, he would be all right. For the moment, at least, there was nothing more that she could do for his parents.

OUT ON THE OCEAN

Trad

The new policeman phoned in sick during the week and then didn't turn up for three more days. He didn't, therefore, come to hear about the latest drama in the village until he presented himself for work on Friday morning. This time there could be no doubt about the case. Thomas O'Neill had joined the ranks of the missing.

He hadn't been seen since Monday, the day that he had met Garda O'Dwyer on the street. The last person who had seen him was his daughter, Mary, who had met him on his way home from the shops. She was on her way into Galway, and he'd asked her to call in for a cup of tea when she got back because, he said, he had something interesting to tell her. But when she got there, three or four hours later, he hadn't been home. Her brother had no idea where he was, and nor had anyone else. Now, four days later, he was still missing. The police had done their work: the harbor had been dragged and the area around the village had been searched. There was no sign, anywhere, of Thomas.

The villagers, already worried, had progressed to a state of panic. They demanded a round-the-clock Garda presence and Sergeant Early promised to supply it. He was less than pleased, therefore, when Larry O'Dwyer arrived in his office at the end of his shift and handed in his notice.

"Why?" he asked him.

"I'm not getting anywhere," said Larry.

"You've only been on the job a few weeks," said Sergeant Early. "Where did you expect to be getting?"

Larry shrugged. "I'm not cut out for it," he said. "I thought it was a good idea to join the guards, but it doesn't seem to be working out the way I expected."

"That's great," said Sergeant Early sardonically. "You have no idea how delighted I am to hear that. Just when we're in the middle of the worst crisis this part of the country has seen in years, you feel, on a personal level, that it's not working out for you."

Larry looked at the floor and counted backward. "Sorry," he said.

"What was it you expected, anyway?" said the sergeant. "High-speed car chases? Gun battles? This isn't America, you know."

"It isn't that," said Larry. "I just thought . . ."

"What did you think?"

"I thought the police knew more than they do. I thought they were good at all kinds of detective work. At least, I think that's what I thought."

Sergeant Early stared at Garda O'Dwyer and wondered if he was quite all there. Maybe the Garda Síochána would, after all, be better off without dreamers like him.

"Whatever you think, Larry," he said. "But it's a good job, you know. What will you do instead?"

"I have plenty to keep me busy," said Larry.

"There's no money to be made out of playing the fiddle, you know."

"I'm not too pushed about money."

"You might think differently if you had a wife and kids to support," said the sergeant.

"I'm sure I would," said Larry.

Sergeant Early sighed and examined the written notice that Larry had given him. The handwriting was large and untidy, like a child's.

"You'll serve out the month, at least?" he said.

"I'll do my best," said Larry.

"Please God we'll have these disappearances sorted out by then," said Sergeant Early.

CONTENTMENT IS
WEALTH

Trad

"You were lucky," said Aengus.

They were sitting on a fallen branch. The goat had gone.

"What was it?" said J.J.

"A púka," said Aengus. "I'm afraid I gave you the wrong advice."

"What do you mean?"

"Well, it was just a joke, really. Don't talk to any goats. I didn't really expect you to meet one."

"So I should have talked to it?"

"Definitely," said Aengus. "He probably thought you were being extremely rude."

"What would he have done to me if you hadn't come along?"

"I've no idea," said Aengus. "But they have powerful

magic, the same púkas. Very old creatures. Much, much older than us. They claim to have been here when the world began. Some of them say that they made it." He thought for a moment, then stretched himself out along the branch, his hands beneath his head. "I probably should have asked him about the leak."

J.J. sighed. His nerves were finally beginning to settle. "So you didn't find anything around here?" he said.

"No," said Aengus. "Not a thing."

J.J. looked around. The woods still frightened him. He was looking forward to getting out of there, but Aengus had closed his eyes and seemed to be having a doze.

"Lesson number five," said J.J. "Have great difficulty in sleeping."

"I'm not sleeping," said Aengus. "We don't do that here."

"You don't sleep?"

"No."

"Never?"

"We usedn't to have a 'never,'" said Aengus. "Or an 'ever.' No night, either." He sat up and looked at the sky. "But I've an awful feeling there's one on the way. What does your watch say?"

J.J. looked at it. "Twenty to seven."

"And what did it say when you arrived?"

"About five thirty."

"Damn," said Aengus, standing up again. "It's getting faster, J.J. It's really getting a grip now."

He picked up the fiddle and began to make his way through the woods, not in the direction of the road, but the other way, toward the top end of the Liddy farmland. J.J. followed him. "How can you tell it's getting faster?" he asked him.

Aengus spoke over his shoulder. "When it first started, we barely noticed it. We had the feeling that something wasn't quite right, but it was so slow there was no way of observing it. Then people began to say that the sun had moved. No one believed them, of course. It couldn't happen. But it was happening. We began to notice shadows where there shouldn't be shadows. Just tiny ones at first, little slivers at the sides of the streets, but they got wider and wider until no one could deny that it was happening anymore. Since then it's been speeding up."

"It's pretty slow compared to my world," said J.J.

"It's still way too fast, though. One of the problems is that we don't know exactly when it started because it was so slow to begin with. If we knew when it all began, in terms of your years, I mean, that might give us a clue as to what's causing it."

"How come?" said J.J.

The moss-covered rocks were slippery underfoot, and the undergrowth was getting thicker. Aengus was struggling to push through hazel and brambles and ash saplings.

"You know the kind of thing," he said. "Earthquakes, hurricanes, nuclear explosions. Always a possibility that something like that could damage the time skin. We've checked out all the obvious ones, but there might have been something we missed."

"Maybe it's something to do with global warming? We've had big changes in the weather lately," said J.J.

"We're not talking about lately, though," said Aengus. "This started long before your time."

"What?"

"The best estimate we can make is somewhere between fifty and a hundred years."

J.J. was having to struggle to keep up with Aengus who, judging by the speed and urgency of his progress through the dense wood, had finally grasped the essentials of worrying.

"Are you telling me that in the time it has taken your sun to move from there"—he pointed—"to there, a hundred years has passed in my world?"

"No," said Aengus. "It might have only been fifty."

The information disturbed J.J. The uneasy feeling that had been nudging at him since he arrived was expanding into something like fear. He still couldn't put his finger on it, though. He knew that some vital piece of knowledge was lodged in his memory, but, like "Dowd's Number Nine," it just wouldn't come to him.

"Where are we going now?" he asked.

They were, finally, coming to the edge of the woods. Aengus pointed to his left, up the steep escarpment at the end of Eagle's Rock. "Up there. I've been trying to put it off, but it has to be done. We're going to pay a visit to my father."

THE PÚKA

Kate Thompson

PART FOUR

To Sergeant Early's annoyance, Garda O'Dwyer didn't turn up for work at all the following week. He phoned the house where he boarded, but the landlady said she hadn't seen him.

"He never spends much time here anyway," she said. "I don't know where he goes."

Sergeant Early put the phone down. "Well, I flaming well know where he goes," he said to Garda Treacy. "He's off playing that blasted fiddle somewhere."

He flung the phone book down on the desk and fixed Treacy with a manic gaze. "They're all the same, you know. Fiddle players. They think they're gods, but they're not. It's the devil's instrument, the fiddle. My father drank himself to death for the love of it, so I should know. It's the devil's instrument."

Ciaran overheard Helen talking on the phone.

"Hi, Phil? It's Helen. . . . Fine, thanks, and you?"

Ciaran knew that she wasn't fine. None of them were. All the talking they had done and all the resignation they had expressed had done nothing to alleviate the gnawing pain of J.J.'s continued absence. It had been more than two weeks now, and it wasn't getting any better. They all detested the much-vaunted concept of "closure," but they were all coming to accept the need for it. Anything would be better than the limbo in which the whole family was existing.

"Have you anything planned for Saturday week?"

Ciaran stood in front of Helen and mimed bewilderment. She had said nothing to him about Saturday week. The days since J.J.'s disappearance had flashed by so fast that there had barely been time for anything beyond the searching of their surroundings. And their minds. And their souls. Ciaran wasn't even sure he knew what day it was.

"We're having a céilí," said Helen, looking at Ciaran, speaking to Phil. "The usual one. Second Saturday."

"What?" said Ciaran.

"Can you and Carol put the word out?" Helen was saying. "Save us the hassle?"

"Helen!" Ciaran hissed.

"J.J. would have wanted it," she said to both of them. "Whatever has happened to him, he's still a Liddy."

SERGEANT EARLY'S JIG

Trad

J.J. stood at the edge of the woods and looked down over the plain. Beneath the clear sky he could make out every detail that lay between the mountainside and the distant sea.

"Can I go down and take a look at my house?" he said to Aengus.

"Later," said Aengus.

"I bet you usedn't to have a 'later,'" said J.J.

He was still looking down the hillside. Where the Liddy house would have been was a stand of tall trees. Their leaves were red, an unexpected fiery blaze on the gray-and-green slopes.

"What kind of trees are those?" J.J. went on, but Aengus had gone. For one of the ever-living ones he was in an unnatural hurry. He was striding across the rough ground toward a series of jagged rock faces, a colossal set of limestone steps that J.J. always avoided climbing if he could. They were easier to scale than the sheer face of Eagle's Rock, but not much.

Bran was lying at his feet. Her loyalty to him was touching, and he wondered where it had sprung from. He was sympathetic to her, but so was Aengus. He was the one who helped her out when the going got too tough for her, not J.J.

"We better follow him, I suppose," he said to her.

But as she heaved herself to her feet, he could see that she was getting weaker. The journey she had already made on three legs was heroic. He couldn't see her getting as far as the top of the mountain.

"Aengus!"

Aengus stopped and waited until they caught up.

"Does your father live up there?" J.J. asked him.

"His house is in the village," said Aengus. "You probably saw it, opposite the pumps."

"You mean the church?" said J.J.

"That's right. But he doesn't live there." Aengus indicated the steep climb ahead of them. "He stays up there."

"Why?" said J.J.

"Because he's contrary," said Aengus. He handed

J.J. the fiddle case and hefted Bran into his arms. Her damaged leg dangled beneath her from its scrap of skin and flesh, swinging with every step that Aengus took. It gave J.J. an idea.

"Aengus?"

Aengus stopped. Despite the weight of the dog and the hard climb, he was hardly out of breath at all.

"Why don't we cut her leg off?"

J.J. wasn't squeamish. He couldn't afford to be, because both Helen and Ciaran were. Animals had accidents all the time around the farm. Usually the vet dealt with them, but there were occasions when it wasn't practical or possible. One of their goats had fallen down a rock face once and damaged a horn so badly that it had been, like Bran's leg, hanging on by a thread. J.J. had cut it off with his penknife.

"There's no saving it," J.J. went on. "She'd do better if she didn't have to drag it along behind her. I've seen dogs before with three legs and they do fine."

"How would we cut if off?" said Aengus.

"I have a knife. I'll do it if you can hold her still."

Aengus looked into the wolfhound's golden eyes. "I don't think she'd like us to do that," he said. "She might misunderstand our intentions."

"It would be over before she knew it," said J.J.

"At your end it might," said Aengus. "I'm not so sure about my end, though. Have you seen her teeth?"

He continued on up the mountainside, and J.J. climbed behind him. He could see the point about the teeth. Bran was a hunting dog and by far the most powerful one he had ever seen. But another idea occurred to him.

"I'll take her with me," he said. "I'll bring her to the vet in the village, give her a bit of time to recover, and then bring her back."

Aengus didn't stop or even turn round, but his words left no room for doubt in J.J.'s mind.

"That, my young ploddy friend, is one thing that you can't do."

THE GREEN
MOUNTAIN

Trad

At the head of the huge steps, Aengus put Bran down, and she followed him and J.J. across the coarse grass of the mountaintop. In three directions they could see the gray Burren hills reaching into the distance, and on the fourth the green plain with the sea beyond. Before long, a huge hill of stones came into sight. In his own world, J.J. had visited it many times. There were two of them on adjacent summits, both so tall that they could be seen from the ocean. They had never been excavated, but it was held that they were burial mounds covering the bones of some ancient royal personage or other.

As they drew closer, J.J. noticed the figure of a man standing on the seaward side of the massive cairn.

"Mind your tongue with this fellow, now," said

Aengus. "He's the Dagda, and he really does think he's a god."

"The what?" said J.J.

"The Dagda," Aengus whispered. "That's his name."

"What does it mean?"

"I haven't the foggiest," said Aengus.

J.J., naturally enough, had expected Aengus's father to be a good deal older than his son, but as they drew closer he was put in mind of the fairy method of rearing their children. The Dagda looked very different; he was bearded, for one thing, and he wore a heavy woollen cloak with a huge gold pin, but he appeared to be only a few years older than his son. He watched them as they approached, but his face showed no emotion.

"Hello, Father," said Aengus.

"Who's the ploddy?"

"His name is J.J.," said Aengus. "But he's not all ploddy. There's a bit of magic in him, isn't there, J.J.? He's a great fiddle player."

"Hmm," said the Dagda, and turned his face toward the sea.

"Father," said Aengus, a little timidly, it seemed to J.J., "we have a bit of a problem."

The Dagda threw back his head in a theatrical gesture and let out an equally theatrical roar of laughter. "A bit of a problem?" he said. "We're all dying, and he calls it a bit of a problem?"

"Dying?" said J.J.

"That's a bit melodramatic, isn't it?" said Aengus.

"Of course we're dying," the Dagda bellowed. "Just as surely as that poor dog there is dying!"

Bran had only just caught up with them, and J.J. had to admit that she didn't look good. She collapsed at his feet and lay straight over on her side in the grass, her tongue lolling out of the side of her mouth. She was panting rapidly.

"A thing is happening that has never happened," the Dagda went on. "Our sun is falling out of our sky. We are dying even as we speak."

"Well, you look all right to me," said J.J.

Aengus grimaced at him, and the Dagda glared at them both.

"He has a point, though," Aengus said. "You call our world the land of eternal youth. What we call your world is . . . well . . ."

"What?" said J.J.

"We call it the land of the dying."

"That's nice of you," said J.J. "Anything has to be better than ploddyland, anyway."

"You are dying from the moment you are born," said the Dagda.

"That may be true," said J.J., "but it isn't the way we choose to look at it."

"It's true all the same," said the Dagda. "And now your filthy time is contaminating—" He broke off and made a sweeping gesture over the plain. "All this. All that is left of us."

There was a silence, broken only by an exhausted groan from the dog.

"All that is left of you?" said J.J.

The Dagda looked out to sea. Aengus put a hand on J.J.'s arm. "Did you not notice?" he said. "How few of us there are?"

J.J. *had* noticed, sort of. He just hadn't registered it. All those empty roads and empty fields and empty houses.

"What happened?" he said.

"You see the beacon?" Aengus indicated the heap of stones. In J.J.'s world, the hill had a little path up one side where people had walked to the top. He'd once had a picnic up there with some of his Dublin cousins. But here there was no path. The stones had an untouched look about them, as though they had just been put there.

"I thought it was a burial mound," he said.

"It may be, in your world," said Aengus. "But not here." He glanced at the Dagda and took a deep breath as though he was beginning a long story. But it wasn't so long.

"When we set out to do battle with your people, hundreds, maybe thousands of years ago now, each of our warriors brought a stone up the mountain and left it here. When the war was over, the ones who survived came back and took their stones away."

J.J. stared at the hill. "So all those people . . ." The scale of it was incomprehensible. If he had to count all those stones it would take him a year.

"All dead," said Aengus.

J.J. looked at the Dagda. Tears were running into his beard.

"But what about the women?" said J.J.

"Our women are warriors, too," said Aengus.

A mile away beyond the hill of stones, on the neighboring peak, J.J. could see its sister beacon. Farther still, he could just make out the tip of a third one. If it existed in his own world, he had never noticed it before. Were there more of them here? Did they line the whole coast of Ireland, awaiting forever the return of the dead souls that had built them?

"Why do you stay here?" he asked the Dagda. "You must know that they'll never come back now."

The Dagda fixed his green gaze on J.J. "I was their commander," he said. "It is not right that I should return and they should not." He turned away and looked out to sea again. "How can I leave them?"

J.J. looked down at Bran. She had recovered a little of her strength and was lying on her belly, her head resting on her outstretched paws. Her eyes were fixed on his face as though she expected something from him.

"I won't let your people die," he said quietly. "If it's the last thing I do, I'll find the leak and stop it."

The Dagda turned back to him. "My fool of a son might be right for once," he said. "Perhaps there is a bit of the sidhe in you after all. Take out that fiddle and play a tune for me." He turned his face toward the beacon. "And for them."

J.J. took out the fiddle and tightened the bow. He had played in some of the top competitions in Ireland and had been heard by some of the best traditional musicians the country had ever produced. But no challenge had been as great as this one: to play for the lost tribes of Tír na n'Óg and their warrior king.

As he lifted the instrument to his shoulder, J.J. knew that his mind would not be a match for this occasion. He had learned, in his years of playing, how it could get in the way if it tried to interfere with the music. He closed it down, felt his soul respond and send his fingers and his bow to the strings. He had played the slow air once through before he knew what it was that he was playing and remembered how it had come down to him, through his mother and his grandmother. There was no doubt in him now, as he played it through again, that the other J.J. Liddy, his great-grandfather, had learned it from the sidhe and knew that he had learned it from them. He might have been playing it now, for all J.J. could tell, because he had never played it like that himself before. And when he came to the end of it, he surprised himself even more, by bursting into a fast, driving reel, and then a second one after it. He had no idea what either of them were called, but he could tell by the smile that slowly dawned on the Dagda's hairy face that he had made good choices. He finished with a flourish and waited expectantly for the Dagda's reaction. But the king of Tír na n'Óg had turned his smile upon his son.

"You're bad news, Aengus Óg," he said. "With all your coming and going, indulging your little fantasies. You're trouble to any poor woman who ever set eyes on you and you're worse trouble to any woman or man who was fool enough to put their trust in you. But you did a thing today that I will not forget in all this dirty time I'm going to be dying in. You brought the right boy with you when you came up the hill."

"I may have, Father," said Aengus, and J.J. saw the familiar flash of anger in his eyes. "But if I did, it wasn't to have him stand here playing tunes for you and your rattling heap of rocks!"

The Dagda let out a roar and whipped a short but lethal-looking sword out from beneath his cloak. "I'll teach you to talk to your father like that!"

"No need," said Aengus. "But that looks like the kind of a useful thing that might take a dog's hind leg off easily enough. Let you hold the end with the teeth and I'll just borrow—"

"That dog is dying!" the Dagda yelled.

"We're all dying, Father. You told us so yourself just two minutes ago. But if we knew where the leak was, we might stop dying."

The Dagda let his arm fall, but he didn't put the sword away. He turned and looked out over the sea once more.

"Father?" said Aengus, his voice concerned, the mischief vanished as quickly as it had appeared. The Dagda made no reply.

"You know, don't you?" said Aengus. "Of course you do. You control the time skin. You know every inch of it. How could you not feel the leak?"

The Dagda continued to stare silently out over the plain.

"It's no good, Father," said Aengus. "It's way too late for you to go down with the ship. You led them to their deaths and there's nothing you can do to change that. Taking yourself and the rest of us with them won't make it any better."

"What was the war about?" said J.J.

Aengus, with difficulty, drew his attention away from his father. "Gods," he said.

"Gods?"

"If you should ever meet me in your world, J.J., don't call me by my name, understand?"

"Why?" said J.J.

"He's afraid you'll blow his cover," said the Dagda.

"I'm afraid that the ploddies will jump to the

wrong conclusions, like they always do," said Aengus. "And start talking about gods walking on the earth. That was what the war was about. Christianity came to Ireland and the ploddies started taking to it. Dad didn't like it. Maintained that he was the god of Ireland. The rest is . . ." He waved his arm at the hill of stones.

J.J. stared at it, trying to take in the full implications of what Aengus had said. A breeze blew up from the sea, cold and fresh. It swayed the Dagda's cloak romantically, but Aengus clearly wasn't impressed.

"Stop it, Dad."

The breeze dropped.

Aengus went on. "If you're so determined to share the fate of your warriors, there's nothing to stop you. All you have to do is go over to the other side. But you don't have the right to drag us all with you. If you know where the leak is, you have to tell us."

The Dagda turned to J.J. "I enjoyed your playing, young lad. I hope you'll come back and play for me again sometime."

It was a regal dismissal. J.J. picked up the fiddle case.

"Dad," said Aengus.

"With or without my amadán son," said the Dagda.

"Where is it, Dad?"

The Dagda looked long and hard at Aengus, then sighed deeply. "I don't know exactly. But it's near here. I can feel it leeching the life from my bones. I can smell it."

"How near?" said Aengus.

"Very near," said the Dagda. "Beneath my feet."

Aengus let out a long sigh of relief. "Right," he said. "Let's go and see if we can find it."

He walked away from his father and the hill of stones. J.J. followed, and Bran struggled to her feet and hobbled along behind them.

THE MOUNTAIN TOP

Trad

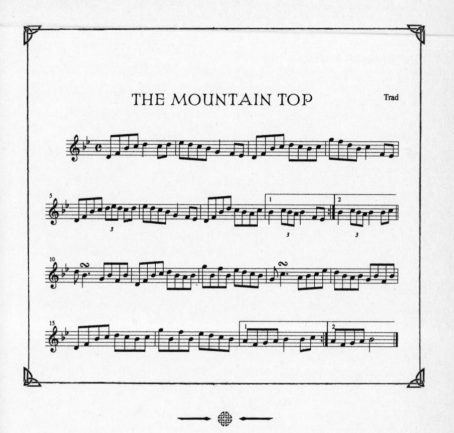

"He gets up my nose," said Aengus. They were climbing back down the jagged corner of the mountain. Bran, unsteadier than ever, was slithering and tumbling down behind them. "It's guilt, you know, that has him up there. It's his fault that we were all but wiped out. Him and his stupid conviction that he's a god."

"I don't know about that," said J.J. "It seems to me that someone who can open and close gates in the sea and the sky can't be far off being a god. Who's going to do it when— if—he dies?"

"If he dies the rest of us won't be far behind him," said Aengus.

"I don't see why you're so pessimistic," said J.J. "We might be ploddies and all, but we've been managing to live with time for thousands and thousands of years. We have children and our children have children and that way we keep going. If you can't get rid of the time, can't you just do the same thing?"

"I've thought about that," said Aengus. "I can't see it happening, though. We've no experience of your kind of life. Even when we're growing up in your world, we don't make a great fist of it. Read the stories and you'll see. We're feckless, dreamy children; we live in a world of our own. And once we get here, well, you can see for yourself. We play music, we dance, we stroll about in the sunshine."

"You could learn, couldn't you?"

"Learn to be like you? We've never had to do anything. We don't know how to grow food or farm cattle or make a living of any kind. We don't know how to look after ourselves, let alone our children."

"You could get people to teach you," said J.J. "I'd help. And I'm sure Anne Korff would."

Aengus nodded. "I know. But there's more to it than that."

He said nothing more, and J.J. sensed a reluctance in him. "Go on," he said at last.

Aengus glanced at him. "We've watched you over the centuries," he said. "If this goes on, we'll start getting hungry. When we stop being hungry, we'll start getting greedy. Can you see us, J.J.? Enslaved by time, driven by greed? Destroying the land that we love? Even if our bloodlines survived, our spirit wouldn't. Industry isn't in our nature, you know? Those future generations would bear no resemblance to us."

"Would it have to be like that?" said J.J. "Couldn't there be another way?"

"If there is," said Aengus, "you haven't found it."

At the edge of the hazel woods, they stopped to let Bran catch up. She was failing badly. J.J. wished there was something he could do for her.

The sun had sunk considerably since J.J. had last observed it, and the light was taking on a golden tinge. He looked out over the placid green plain.

"What did the Dagda mean when he accused you of indulging your little fantasies?" he asked Aengus.

Aengus spat derisively. "I've been going over to your side to have a look around, that's all. The trouble is, it's not always easy to remember what you're doing there."

"Anne Korff said something like that," said J.J. "Why is that?"

"Don't know," said Aengus. "Something to do with

the time shock to the brain, I suppose. You can wind up being a bit vague about things." He shook his head. "Bit rich, though, him accusing me of indulging fantasies. I'm not the one with the god complex!"

"I feel sorry for him," said J.J.

"He'd be delighted to hear you say that," said Aengus. "Tell him when you next meet him."

"But it's awful, what happened to your people."

"Truly terrible," said Aengus. "But it's happened. Nothing can change it. It's too late for the Dagda to decide it wasn't a great idea."

"What do you think he should do, then?"

Aengus smiled. "You should see my father dance, J.J. He should come down off the mountain and live with his people." He reflected for a moment, then added, "Or die with them."

J.J. was irritated with Aengus. It was all very well to be scornful of the Dagda and to criticize the ploddies and accuse them of being greedy. What entitled him and the others to drift around in perpetual bliss while on the other side of the time skin people slaved and died and suffered all the troubles associated with mortality?

But the leak wasn't only affecting Tír na n'Óg. He had almost forgotten why he had come. If time was gaining such momentum here, what might be happening back there?

He looked at his watch. Quarter to seven. In a while longer, time in this world would be matching that in his own world for speed.

"We'd better do something," he said.

"The leak," said Aengus.

They looked at the rock-strewn hillside below them. There was no obvious choice of direction.

"Do you mind if we go down that way?" said J.J. "That's my house down there in the trees. I'd like to see what it looks like over here."

"I suppose we may as well," said Aengus. "I've no better idea, anyway."

They walked down the steep hill toward the farmhouse. The same hill was their winterage at home, but here there were no walls, and although J.J. recognized individual rocks and some of the shapes that were in the land, he was slightly disoriented and couldn't quite get his bearings.

About halfway down to the house he stopped and looked back, trying to place his position in the landscape. That was it. There had been no clearance here, no bulldozing. They had already come past the top meadow with its ring fort, but here, along with a lot of the other fields, it was still covered with rock.

He had his bearings now, but something else was missing.

"Where's Bran?"

Aengus stopped and looked around. "I don't know." He called her.

J.J. called as well. "Bran? Here, girl."

They waited, but the dog didn't appear.

"Oh, no," said J.J. "I hope she hasn't given up."

"She could be stuck somewhere," said Aengus. "Did we climb over any big rocks?"

"I don't think so," said J.J. "I'd better go back and look for her."

"I'll wait for you," said Aengus.

KING OF THE FAIRIES

Trad

Ciaran had tried to talk Helen out of holding the céilí, but she wouldn't be dissuaded. What was more, she had their daughter's full backing. Marian was not going to dance, though, this time. She was ready to take J.J.'s place, playing at her mother's side.

Time was still racing away from them all. They made no efforts to compensate themselves for J.J.'s absence with any kind of distraction, but even so their days flew by with impossible speed. It was almost as though the hours were being leeched away by some vast, unseen vacuum. And with every one that passed, the prospect of J.J. returning grew dimmer.

Sergeant Early had written off the new policeman. He hadn't turned up for days. It vaguely crossed his mind that there might be another case of a disappearance, but he was not inclined to investigate. If O'Dwyer had disappeared, it was, at least, one less headache for him to deal with.

They were getting nowhere with the missing persons. Reluctantly, they had accepted that Anne Korff would have to be included in the tally. It was more than a fortnight now since she had locked up her house and gone, and she hadn't made contact with anyone yet. Special detectives had been drafted in from Dublin, and the whole round of house-to-house inquiries had been repeated. Nothing, absolutely nothing was emerging.

When Garda O'Dwyer did turn up for work, just in time to go out on night duty, Sergeant Early roasted him. O'Dwyer weathered the storm of abuse by gazing fixedly at the wall and counting backward from a hundred. It was well for the sergeant that he did. He had no inkling of what the new policeman might have done to him had he lost his temper. When the tirade was finally over, Larry refocused himself and accepted the orders he was given for the night. As he left the office he said to Sergeant Early, "I hear you play the banjo. A gorgeous instrument. We must get a tune together some time."

He was posted in Gort, for the happy hours after the pubs closed. There were some rough elements in the town, and there was plenty to keep him busy that particular night. Larry was not averse to making difficult arrests, or even to jumping on a few heads, though he could think of several better ways of dealing with miscreants. All the same it was not, as far as he could remember, the reason that he had become a policeman.

Helen was taken by surprise on her birthday. She was working so hard at just carrying on that she had forgotten all about it. Ciaran and Marian woke her with breakfast in bed and a pile of presents so big that it took her half an hour to open them all. They made her stay in bed while they did the morning jobs, but she had to get up when friends started calling with more presents.

Ciaran cooked lunch. Afterward he announced that they were all going to the pictures in Ennis, and from there to a meal in Helen's favorite Chinese restaurant. The day flew by and Helen entered into the spirit of it as well as she could, but they all knew that her pleasures were hollow without J.J. there to share them. As they were about to set out for the cinema, she said,

"What if he comes back and there's nobody here?"

"He'll wait," said Ciaran. "What else would he do?"

But Helen wasn't happy with that. Before they left, she wrote a note for him and left it out on the kitchen table.

THE ANGRY PEELER

Trad

J.J. retraced his steps across the hillside. He called out to Bran again and again, but she didn't come, and locating a gray dog in terrain that was predominantly gray was beginning to look like an impossible task.

She couldn't be that far away. She had been with them at the bottom of the stony steps, and he was fairly sure that she had started out with them as they came down the hill. Dead or alive, he was sure to come across her if he kept looking for long enough.

Still calling, he climbed up to the edge of the hazel and looked in. The shadows were deep in there, and although J.J. couldn't see anything that looked like a goat, he had no intention of going in without Aengus.

"Bran? Bran!"

But if Bran was in the hazel woods, she wasn't coming out.

From his vantage point J.J. looked back down the hillside. Despite the overall grayness, he was fairly sure that she wasn't anywhere within sight. Aengus Óg wasn't visible either, and J.J. assumed he must have gone on to the house. As far as J.J. could see, there was only one place where Bran could be concealed from view, and that was in the ring fort. Its outline was quite clear, but he could see little within its circumference because of the holly and whitethorn growing there. He walked back down to it and stepped over the low wall of standing stones.

There was still no sign of the dog. J.J. walked between the trees, calling as he went. The inside of the rath was exactly as his own one was at home, tree for tree and stone for stone. But as he came to the middle, J.J. saw that there was one major difference. Where in his world there was just another pile of stones breaking the surface, here there was a place where a flat stone seemed to have slipped sideways and was hanging on its edge, almost as though it was hinged. Beneath it was a deep hole. J.J. kneeled down and peered into it. Underneath the flat stone, the hole broadened out.

It was, without doubt, the entrance to a souterrain.

As he looked down into it, J.J. heard sounds, muffled by their passage from the depths of the earth. He slithered down into the hole, noticing as he did so the fresh scratches of a dog's claws and a damp smear of blood.

"Bran?"

He listened, and heard more distinctly now the low, menacing snarling of a dog and a man's voice, raised in anger. A swift chill ran through J.J.'s veins. Down there in the darkness was something he was in no hurry to investigate. He scrambled back to the surface and ran to the edge of the fort.

He couldn't see Aengus. He shouted his name. It bounced around among the rocks for a while, but wherever Aengus was, it didn't reach him. J.J. yelled again, louder. There was no reply.

J.J. was frightened. He was out of his depth, and Aengus Óg had done a bunk. With no clear idea about what he was going to do, he went back to the mouth of the souterrain. Down there in the darkness, Bran was still growling. There was a shout and a bark, a moment of silence, then he heard her growling again.

"Bran!" He waited. She wasn't going to come. Why had she gone down there and who had she found?

She had followed him so determinedly wherever he had gone in Tír na n'Óg. Him, not Aengus. He didn't know why, but he was certain that she had purposefully attached herself to him as soon as she'd seen him walking down the main street of the village. It made no sense that she didn't respond to his call.

Unless she couldn't. It was that thought, the sudden realization that Bran might be in danger, that galvanized J.J. into overcoming his fear. With unsteady hands, he unzipped his inside pocket and took out the candle and matches.

The bright flame in front of his face blinded him as he wriggled through the crawl hole. Anything might have hit him as he lifted his head on the other side, but nothing did. The first hall was empty; the only movement came from the flickering shadows created by his candle. The sounds were clearer, though, and as he walked through the long, narrow room, he began to hear words.

"Go on! Go back! Get out of here!"

Bran, then, was the aggressor. But why? Who was she threatening? J.J. became a little more curious and a little less afraid. The dog was in a bad way, but as Aengus had pointed out, there was nothing wrong with her teeth. Weak as she was, she wouldn't let anyone harm him as long as she had the use of them.

He kneeled down and squeezed through into the second chamber. The light from his candle revealed the burly shape of the wolfhound just beyond the entrance. She swayed and wobbled, barely able to stay on her feet, but her snarls were savage enough to be taken seriously by anyone who heard them. She had not registered his arrival, and even though he knew her, he was reluctant to reach out a hand. Her attention was fixed on the opposite corner of the chamber, where the man was standing.

"Call off your hellhound!" he shouted.

J.J. held up his candle and nearly dropped it in surprise. The man was wearing black clothes and a dog collar. For reasons known only to herself, Bran was engaged in a standoff with a priest.

THE PRIEST WITH
THE COLLAR

Trad

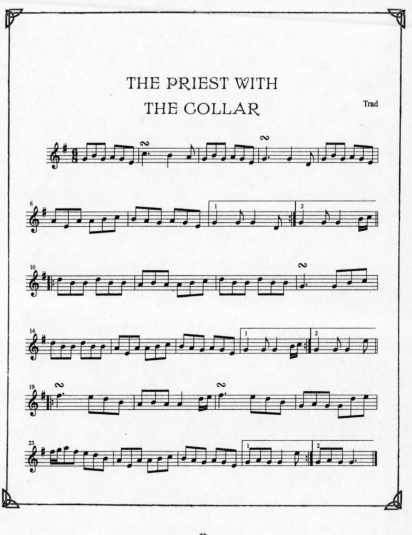

"Call him off!" said the priest.

J.J. had never yet given Bran an order. For one thing, she wasn't his dog. For another, she had been born a millennium or two before him, and what that might mean in terms of seniority he hadn't worked out. But he could see why the priest was so upset. She was being very aggressive.

"Bran!" he said. "Stop!"

She glanced at him and dropped, with relief or resignation, onto her belly. Her snarls diminished and died away, but she was still watching the priest with a keen eye.

"Put her out," he said.

J.J. considered the situation. The priest was an older man, in his sixties at least. He was shorter than

J.J. and lighter. He looked much more frightened than frightening, and J.J.'s curiosity was getting the better of his nerves.

"Out, Bran," he said as convincingly as he could. She looked up at him with pleading eyes.

"I mean it. Out!"

She was desperately weak. It was all she could do to haul herself to her feet and wobble slowly out through the crawl hole. J.J. heard her claws clicking on the stones and the little grunt she gave as she lay down on the other side of the wall. He lifted the candle and stepped forward into the room.

"Who are you?" said the priest.

J.J. didn't answer. His eye had fallen on something, and his attention was riveted. Behind the shadowy figure of the priest, at about the height of his hip, something was jutting out of the wall. At first glance it looked like a stick or a branch, but already, even in the dim light cast by the priest's candle, J.J. could see that it wasn't. It was too regular and smooth; someone had shaped it like that. It was hollow, and it had a small hole in the side. More than one.

It was a flute.

The sudden rush of understanding felt like a landslide in J.J.'s brain. He knew whose flute it was and who had made it. He knew who the priest was; he even knew his name. And he knew how time was leaking into Tír na n'Óg. The time skin was sealed quite perfectly around the barrel of the flute, but the flute was hollow. The membrane could not reach the bore.

J.J.'s first instinct was to pull it out. He took a step forward, but the priest moved to the side and blocked his way.

"Who are you?" he said again.

J.J. was tempted to rush him. He was sure he could do it; grab the flute and be gone with it before the older man could stop him. Even if it came to a struggle, he could probably come out on top. But something restrained him. His great-grandfather, the first J.J. Liddy, could have done the same thing all those years ago; he could have used his youth and superior strength to reclaim his flute. He hadn't done it. J.J. wouldn't either. He would find another way.

"Are you deaf?" said Father Doherty.

"No. My name's J.J." He knew better than to confuse the issue by giving his great-grandfather's name. "J.J. Byrne," he finished up.

"J.J. Byrne," said the priest, eyeing him carefully. J.J. noticed that he paid particular attention to his blue-

and-white sneakers. "That's a strange name for a fairy."

"It would be," said J.J. "But then, I'm not a fairy."

"Well, you have the manners of one," the priest snapped.

"Sorry, Father," said J.J. He went to mass with his parents every Sunday morning. He had plenty of respect for priests in general, but not this one.

"If you're not a fairy, then what are you doing here?"

J.J. thought hard. He had no intention of telling Father Doherty why he was here, and to say that he had been introduced to Tír na n'Óg by a local publisher wouldn't sound terribly convincing. A groaning sigh from Bran on the other side of the crawl hole inspired him.

"I followed my dog down a hole," he said. "And now we're trying to get home."

Father Doherty's response was unexpected. He stepped up close to the wall, laid a possessive hand on the end of the flute, and gestured toward the corner. "Off you go then."

J.J. grasped at straws. "But that's a stone wall," he said.

The priest smiled. "It looks like a stone wall, but it isn't. Have faith, child. Trust me." When J.J. still hung back, he went on, "You may think you can't get out at the other end, but you can. There are big stones in the entrance, but there is a light flagstone in one corner. There was one here as well, but I suppose your dog must have disturbed it. You will find it lifts easily, and there's plenty of room for you to climb out."

J.J. felt trapped. He could still make a lunge for the flute and wrestle it away from the priest, but it had to be a last resort.

"But what about you, Father?" he asked. "What are you doing down here?"

Father Doherty smiled and sat down on a large stone beside the wall. His hand was still resting on the flute, and J.J. got the impression that he was very much accustomed to that posture, as if he had spent a great deal of time sitting in it.

"I have to stay a bit longer," he said, "but I shall be leaving here shortly as well."

"Why do you have to stay?" said J.J. "What's that you're doing with the flute?"

Father Doherty smiled, more to himself than to J.J. "Stroke of genius, wasn't it, to use the flute? I am achieving a lifetime's ambition, J.J. Byrne. I am ridding Ireland of the fairies and their insidious ways forever."

"Why?" J.J. wanted to keep him talking while he worked out what to do next. It was proving easy enough to do.

"They have been the bane of Irish life for generation upon generation. They corrupt the people's minds with their music and their dancing and their deceitful ways. Don't you agree?"

"I don't really know too much about them, Father. But I'm sure you must be right."

"They have turned the Irish people into an idle race full of fanciful dreaming and heathen superstitions. They have even corrupted our blood, J.J. Did you know that?"

"I didn't, Father."

"They steal our children and leave their own brats in their cradles. And that's not the worst thing they do. They walk abroad among us, J.J., in the broad light of day. Their menfolk charm our girls with their seductive ways and then leave them to bear the consequences of their mortal sins."

J.J. wasn't sure he understood that last bit. The priest enlightened him.

"Children born out of wedlock, child. There are those among us even now who are tainted with the blood of the sidhe."

He fell silent for a moment, seeming to lose himself in the flame of his candle, which sat in a puddle of its own wax on the ground. "I have a vision for Ireland," he went on. "I see a God-fearing Catholic nation peopled by industrious citizens, each one of them determined to put the old, feckless ways behind them. I see an Ireland where every man has a motorcar and spends his time improving his lot and the lot of his family, instead of wasting his days growing potatoes and his nights drinking and dancing. I see an Ireland that has grown wealthy and taken its rightful place among the great states of Europe."

"But all that has happened already," said J.J.

"Already?" said Father Doherty.

"You should see Ireland now, Father. No one sees fairies anymore. They don't even believe in them."

"Are you telling me the truth?" said the priest.

"I am, Father," said J.J. He didn't feel that he was lying. Most of what Father Doherty had envisaged really had come true.

"I didn't expect it to happen so soon," said the priest. He looked closely at J.J. again, and his eyes came to rest on his sneakers. "What year is it, child?"

J.J. told him. The priest's eyes lost focus. He repeated the year, and J.J. sensed a sadness in him as he said it. "Who would have guessed that time could move so fast over there?"

"So perhaps you don't need to stay any longer?" said J.J.

But Father Doherty shook his head. He took a large fob watch out of his pocket and held it to the light. "Another three hours," he said. "That's all I need."

"J.J.?"

Priest and boy froze, their eyes locked together as the voice boomed down through the hollow halls.

"Who's that?" whispered the priest.

"Aengus Óg," said J.J., unable to think of anything else to say.

"Keep him out!" hissed Father Doherty urgently.

J.J. scrabbled through the first crawl hole and called up from the next one. "I'm here, Aengus. I'll be out in a minute. Wait there for me."

Back inside again, he whispered to Father Doherty, "Why do you need another three hours?"

The priest was clearly terrified of Aengus Óg. His voice trembled as he answered. "Night. I have to stay until night falls."

"Why?"

Father Doherty released the flute and made a

swift, pulling motion above it. "I pull it out."

J.J. stared at him, trying to work out the significance of what he was saying.

"Time stops again," he went on. "Forever. Eternal night in Tír na n'Óg." He laughed, which isn't easy to do in a terrified whisper. "That will put an end to them, don't you think?"

J.J. didn't know what to think. "But Father, surely that will make them all come over into our world?"

"It might," said the priest. "In which case they will die, just as you and I will die. And then they will have to atone to their Maker for their century upon century of sins."

"J.J.?" Aengus sounded closer this time.

"Keep him out!"

"I can't, Father," said J.J., grasping at a sudden inspiration. "But I think your watch must be slow."

"What?"

"It's already dark, Father."

"Is it?"

"Look." J.J. pressed the time-zone button on his watch and hoped for the best. He put his wrist beside the candle. It had worked. He turned the watch face toward the priest. "It's a quarter past eleven."

"The Lord be praised," said Father Doherty.

"What are you up to in there?" Aengus was at the crawl hole. Another moment and he would be in there with them.

"Quick," said Father Doherty. "Follow me."

He pulled the flute out of the membrane, paused for an instant to cross himself, then stepped through. At the last possible moment, J.J. made a grab for the flute and prepared to hang on tight. As the time skin closed behind the priest, there was a slight resistance on the other end and then it was gone. J.J. held his great-grandfather's flute in his hand.

The time leak had stopped.

AFTER THE SUN GOES
DOWN

Trad

PART FIVE

In the Chinese restaurant, Helen experienced a sudden release of pressure, as though a weight that she had been struggling beneath for years had unexpectedly been removed from her. She took a deep breath and looked at the others. They were looking at her quizzically as though they too had felt something. All three of them breathed a deep sigh and relaxed in their chairs. Looking round the restaurant, they noticed other customers doing the same thing.

They had been worried that there wouldn't be time for a decent meal before they had to get back for the evening milking, but now, when Ciaran looked at his watch, he saw that there was plenty of time.

"Dessert, anyone?" he said.

❂ ❂ ❂

Across the length and breadth of Ireland, and way, way beyond it, the same sense of relief was felt. Those who talked about synchronicity and similar intangible things would continue to talk about that day for years to come. Those who were silent in regard to such matters were not beyond noticing it either, and even the scientists had something to say about it. They were yet to be introduced to the existence of Tír na n'Óg and the potentially lethal effect of flutes, and thus they proved, beyond any measure of doubt, that an actual change in the speed of time was outside the realms of possibility. They put it down to an obscure "hundredth monkey" phenomenon; an inexplicable but welcome change in the psyche of the species. Much as some of them might have wished to, the one thing they could not do was deny that a change had taken place. They experienced, along with the rest of the population of the planet, a sudden and dramatic increase in time in their day-to-day lives.

Everyone adjusted rapidly, though few forgot the nightmare days of the past when the hours had flown past like snowflakes in a blizzard. No one could understand how they could have allowed it to happen. There was plenty of time. There must always have been plenty of time. They must have used it wrongly, that was all. Adults took up old hobbies or revisited forgotten childhood passions. Hand-knitted sweaters and gloves and scarves came back into fashion. Workplaces got on schedule, many of them for the first time ever, and employees and management alike discovered that there was room in their lives for their families as well as their jobs.

As for the children, they found that there was, after all, time for more in a day than school, homework, and washing up. There was time for reading books as well as watching telly. There was time to mooch along country lanes; time to pick an ash plant and wallop the heads off stinging nettles; time to pop the big white bindweed flowers out of their little green beds. There was time to mix mud with orange juice to see what it would make; time to stand in puddles and watch the water go in over their shoes; time to stay out in the rain until they got really, *really*, REALLY wet. And none of it mattered now, because there was time for their parents to make them hot milk and dress them in warm pajamas and tell them a bedtime story that went on and on and on until finally it became part of their dreams.

THE RAINY DAY

Trad

In Tír na n'Óg, the effects were no less dramatic. On the quay the musicians felt the shift and stopped playing. The dancers looked at the sky, looked at one another, let out a roar of delight. The music started again, but Anne Korff was remembering the advice she had given to J.J. Liddy on his way into Tír na n'Óg and hoped that he would not forget. She hoped that she would not forget it either, between here and the nearest souterrain. She separated herself, not without difficulty, from the euphoric crowd and started out for home. But on the way up the main street of the village, she met Séadna Tobín standing on the footpath laughing at the alchemy shop. He had, she noticed, his fiddle with him. It would be nice to have someone to walk home with. And if he wanted to stay for a tune or two first, what harm?

As they went back down toward the quay they met the goat coming the other way, with Devaney not far behind.

"Head her off, will you?" he called, but it was already too late. She had dodged past them and was skittering off up the street, her dainty feet drumming on the cobbles.

DEVANEY'S GOAT

Trad

Inside the souterrain, Aengus and J.J. felt the change as well, and it was absolutely wonderful. It was like the end of an illness or the delivery of a new baby, or the return home after a long, long absence. But their pleasure in the moment was ruined by a dreadful throaty rattle that came from Bran. J.J. hurried through the crawl hole, closely followed by Aengus.

The dog was lying flat on her side. Her breath was coming in short, ragged gasps, and as J.J. laid a hand on her shoulder, he found that her whole body was rigid with tension.

"Oh, Bran," he said. "Come on, girl. You saved Tír na n'Óg, you know. You can't go and die on us."

"She won't," said Aengus solemnly. "There's no chance of that now."

But J.J. was a farmer. He had seen his share of dying animals. "I wish you were right," he said, "but I don't think you are."

"What happened in there, J.J.?"

J.J. tore his attention away from the dog. "It was a priest. Father Doherty." He held up the flute. "He had this pushed through the wall."

"Ah," said Aengus. "So that's what became of the old lad."

"How did you know about him?" said J.J.

"I met him on a few occasions," said Aengus.

"Where?"

"Here and there," said Aengus. "He spent his whole life coming and going, getting to know us, trying to persuade us to stay out of his parish; his world, in fact. I should have suspected that he'd try and find a way of keeping us out. Pretty clever idea he had. I have to give him that."

J.J. laughed. "I wonder what he'll make of modern Ireland? What's going to happen if he finds out that I cheated him and comes back? Do you think he'll try again?"

"No," said Aengus. "I'm certain that he won't."

He turned and started to crawl back into the inner chamber.

"Where are you going?" said J.J.

"I just have a little fantasy to indulge," said Aengus, disappearing from sight.

"Are you going through?" J.J. called.

Aengus didn't answer. J.J. stroked Bran's head. "Maybe we should go with him. What do you think?"

But Aengus didn't appear to have gone anywhere. He came back through the crawl hole with the priest's little stump of a candle. "Shall we get out of here?" he said.

It took both of them to carry the heavy dog out of the souterrain and up to the surface. In the daylight she looked no better.

"I'm sure she's dying," said J.J.

"She is," said Aengus. "But she won't die."

Slowly the realization dawned upon J.J. "She won't get better but she won't get worse." It was Drowsy Maggie who had said it. Bran had gotten worse, because of the time that was leaking into Tír na n'Óg. But now . . .

Now. That was all there was. Now.

"J.J.," said Aengus gently. "You know, don't you, that Bran didn't go down into the souterrain because Father Doherty was there. She's a dog. She had no idea what we were doing, wandering round the hills and dales. She attached herself to you because you're a ploddy and she thought you might lead her to an open gate. You didn't, so she found one herself. Animals can sense them, you know, especially ones that have come and gone as much as she has. I suppose you'd call it an instinct."

"But why?" said J.J. "Why did she want to go through?"

Aengus ran his hand along the dog's matted coat. "She came here to escape her death. We don't know what happened to her, but you can see how badly injured she is. Just in time, she found a gate and came through. Her life here wasn't exactly comfortable, but to her it was preferable to dying. Until the leak began."

J.J. nodded. "When time got in, she began to get worse."

"That's right," said Aengus. "And eventually her life became intolerable to her. She no longer wanted to avoid her death. She wanted to go back and meet it."

Bran gave a feeble groan and shuddered, stiffly. J.J. felt a flash of anger. "We could have saved her from this," he said. "You should have let me take her through to the vet before she got this bad."

"But you couldn't have, J.J. I told you that already."

J.J. looked at him blankly.

"Oh, dear," said Aengus. "I thought you understood. Surely you can't have forgotten what happened to Oisín?"

THE NEW CENTURY

Trad

It was the new policeman who found the body in the souterrain. He wasn't even on duty at the time, but was doing a bit of sniffing around on his own initiative. Sergeant Early ate him again for missing another three days' work, but he was pleased with him all the same. At least they had something to show for all that Garda effort.

Not that it had any bearing on the missing persons. The police made that clear from the very beginning, but nevertheless, rumors spread like wildfire. O'Dwyer was sent to his lodgings to collect his uniform and posted in the little Garda station in the village, where he fielded anxious questions all day. He gave little away. The body was in a very advanced state of decay when it was found, and would appear to have been there for many, many years. Forensic teams were investigating the souterrain and would remove the body for postmortem. It would be a few days before any attempt could be made at identification.

But that was enough information for most people round there. By the end of the day, the village knew that an old mystery had been brought back into the daylight. It had to be Father Doherty.

It was widely agreed that this was proof of his murder by old J.J. Liddy. The souterrain was on his land. Who else would have known that it existed? It was a perfect place for a murderer to hide a corpse. No one said as much to Helen, of course, but it was difficult even for her to put any other interpretation on the discovery. On top of her son's disappearance, it was a blow that she found crippling.

There could no longer be any question of holding the céilí that was planned for the following day. Helen left it to Ciaran to phone around and cancel it. For the first time in the month since J.J. went missing, she allowed her depression to get the better of her and took herself off to bed.

It was midday on Saturday before she got up again. Ciaran and Marian had milked the goats and turned them out into a day that was alternating between bright sunshine and heavy showers. They were in the kitchen playing a game of cards when Helen came down.

"It's true, isn't it?" she said. "About Father Doherty."

"They haven't identified him yet," said Ciaran.

"They will," said Helen. "It's him. I was just hoping it might all have been a dream."

Ciaran stood up and put his arms around her, but she moved away from him, shifted the kettle onto the hottest plate of the range, and stood with her back to its warmth.

"Are you doing anything this afternoon, Maz?" she said.

Marian had lots to do, but there was plenty of time for all of it. "Nothing in particular," she said.

"I'm going to make a start on some cheese," said Helen. "After that, if you felt like it, I might teach you a couple of tunes."

MY MIND WILL NEVER
BE EASY

Trad

J.J. stared at the dying dog. Once again he was experiencing that sense of a landslide in his brain. But this time it hurt.

Of course he remembered Oisín. He was Fionn Mac Cumhail's son, who fell in love with a woman of the sidhe and went to live in Tír na n'Óg. He was happy there—here—until he got a yearning to see his beloved Ireland again. His friends in Tír na n'Óg advised him against it, and when he insisted on going they lent him a white horse and warned him that he must never get down from its back as long as he was in Ireland.

When he got there, Oisín found that hundreds of years had passed. Everything had changed. He knew no one and no one knew him. He stayed on his horse, but he encountered a group of men trying to move a huge rock that was in the middle of a field. They asked for his help, and when he leaned from the horse to put a hand to the rock, he slipped and fell. The moment he touched the soil of Ireland, he disintegrated into dust.

J.J. looked up at Aengus. "So that's why I couldn't take her to the vet?"

"He couldn't have done much for a heap of dust."

Another awful realization slithered in on the heels of the last one. "And . . . and Father Doherty?"

"A pile of dry bones," said Aengus.

J.J. thought about it. "I tricked him, Aengus," he said. "He wanted to stay until it got dark, but I told him it was dark already."

"Good lad," said Aengus, sounding genuinely impressed. "I always said you weren't all ploddy."

"But don't you understand? I sent him through to his death. I killed him."

"You did not," said Aengus. "That man knew more about this world than I do. He knew what he was doing."

"But he can't have. He couldn't have gone through the wall knowing that he would be dead by the time he got to the other side."

"Why not?" said Aengus. "He hated Tír na n'Óg and its people. He wouldn't have wanted to stay here. He was a man of the cloth, J.J. I'm sure he expected to walk straight into another kind of eternity and find great favor with his Father up there. And who knows? Maybe he has."

J.J. looked across the plains to the sea. The whole vista glowed in the soft light. Unless someone else like Father Doherty came along, this was the way Tír na n'Óg would stay, basking forever in this warm, golden evening.

"I'd better go home."

"You're free to do as you like," said Aengus, "but I'd advise against it."

"Why?"

"What makes you think you're any different from Oisín and Bran and Father Doherty?"

"But that's ridiculous," said J.J. "I've only been here—" He stopped. That was the whole point. No time passed here. A thousand years could go by in Ireland, but here it was always now. The dreadful truth dawned upon J.J.

"Look on the bright side," said Aengus Óg. "You can stroll around in the sunshine. You can learn some new tunes, and I hear you're a great dancer as well."

"But what about my parents?" said J.J.

"Don't worry about them. They'll miss you for a dance or two, and then they'll forget all about you."

"No, they won't. We're not like you, Aengus. We don't live in the eternal present. We don't forget."

"Oh," said Aengus. "Well. Too bad. Chances are they're long gone by now anyway. Ploddies don't last, you know."

"Don't say that!" said J.J. "It can't be true."

Aengus reached out and tousled J.J.'s hair affectionately. "Come on," he said. "Don't let it get you down. There's nothing you can do, so you may as well forget about it. You belong here. You're one of us." An idea struck him. "Can you play that yoke?"

J.J. looked at the flute. He had forgotten it was there. One end of it was blackened and dusty from seventy years of exposure to the souterrain in his own world. The other was as clean and shiny as when his great-grandfather had last played it. He didn't want to forget his parents and his predicament, but the truth is that few can resist the subtle powers that the land of eternal youth has over the people who find their way to it.

Perhaps Aengus was right? Perhaps there was nothing that J.J. could do? He pulled up a handful of grass and rubbed the grime and cobwebs off the flute. The wood had been so well tempered by its years as the spoke of a cartwheel that it had not suffered at all from its time in the wall. J.J. lifted it to his mouth and blew into it. There was nothing in it but whistles and wheezes.

Aengus had the fiddle out. "Try again," he said.

More wheezes and squeaks. And then, or now, a clear, mellow note. J.J.'s fingers moved instinctively, picking out a few short phrases and arpeggios. He had never heard anything like the tone that was beginning to emerge. No wonder his great-grandfather had loved it so much.

"That's a great flute, J.J.," said Aengus. "The best I ever heard."

As J.J. continued warming up the old instrument, Aengus adjusted the fiddle's tuning to it. He began a jig. After a few more unintentional whistles, J.J. found the tone again and took up the tune. But he was uneasy. His eye fell on Bran, trapped in her death throes for eternity. It was awful, but what was the use in him worrying about her and empathizing with her pain? Why should he cause himself distress when there was nothing, absolutely nothing, that he could do about it?

So he played, one well-loved tune after another, and forgot about everything except the music. He looked up, caught Aengus's eye, and felt his spirits soar. It's impossible to smile while you're playing the flute, so J.J. raised his eyebrows instead and threw in an overblow for a few notes, which made the flute hop up an octave. Aengus whooped with delight and responded with a series of ingenious variations.

With a glance and a nod they changed to a new tune. The two instruments blended perfectly, and the wild, thrilling music rang out over the beautiful land where it had been born.

FAR FROM HOME

Trad

"Will we go down to the village?" said Aengus. "See if Devaney caught the goat yet?"

"I don't see why he has to catch her," said J.J. "Why can't he just turn her into a bodhrán from a distance?"

"He did that once. The bodhrán rolled away down the hill and into the sea. He had to go over beyond until it dried out. . . . He says she did it to him on purpose. He says it's never been the same since."

"It sounds pretty good to me," said J.J.

He took the fiddle, and Aengus hefted the dog into his arms. Together they picked their way down the hillside above the stand of strange red trees where, in his own world, J.J.'s house stood. Aengus began to track to his right, toward the mountain road, but J.J. still wanted to see the place.

"Do you mind?" he asked.

Aengus looked irritated. "It's just that the dog's a bit heavy."

"You can go on if you like, and I'll catch you up. I won't be long." He laughed. "In fact, I won't be any time at all."

But when he walked down to the edge of the copse, Aengus went with him. The red trees were tall, with broad trunks and dense, crinkly leaves.

"What are they?" J.J. asked.

"Chiming maple," said Aengus. "That's what they were known as in your world, anyway. The last one over there was cut down in 1131."

"Really? Why?"

"The wood has amazing acoustic properties. Your early churches and minstrel galleries were all lined with it. It had the effect of turning the whole building into a musical instrument. Beautiful," he said, remembering. "But like all the most wonderful things, it was too much in demand. It made the best musical instruments as well. We call it the bell tree."

J.J. put his hand on the nearest red trunk.

"Play a few notes there under it," said Aengus.

J.J. lifted the flute and began to play a tune. The whole tree resonated in sympathy, filling the air with sweet, ringing harmonies.

"Wow," he said.

"There's a guy in your world making fiddles from it," said Aengus. "He sends one of his apprentices over now and then to get the wood. He lives in Italy, I think. Tony, that's it. Tony Stradivarius."

"Not Antonius Stradivarius?" said J.J. incredulously.

"That's him. I used to have one of his fiddles. I left it behind me somewhere. . . ."

"But he's been dead for over two hundred years," said J.J.

"Oh. Has he?" said Aengus. "It's hard to keep track. . . . You're a lot better off over here, you know."

J.J. played to the tree again, then stopped and listened to the resonances.

"I knew a lovely girl once," Aengus went on. "I was mad about her, actually. But I went back to visit her again and . . . well . . . it was awful. You ploddies just don't last."

J.J. was only half listening. It was all very well for Aengus. He could come and go as he pleased between the worlds. It didn't seem fair that J.J. was stuck here forever.

He walked in among the trees. In their midst was a cottage, very much like the others he had seen here;

more like a hollowed-out lump of rock than a house. It appeared to be quite empty, and he had no inclination to go in. He wandered around the outside, but there was nothing to connect this edifice with the house where he had been born. Nothing, that was, until he came to the spot where the new extension would be standing. There, against the trunk of another of the maple trees, was a little drift of very familiar socks.

He was still there when Aengus came looking for him. "Haven't you seen enough?"

"Yes," said J.J. He was following Aengus away from the house when he heard, or thought he heard, music. He turned back and bent his head toward the small, dark doorway. It was faint, but it was definitely there.

"What is it?" said Aengus.

"Music," said J.J.

"Oh, I doubt it," said Aengus. "Come on. Let's go."

"No. I can definitely hear it. There must be a leak here."

"You didn't believe all that nonsense, did you?" said Aengus. "You can't really hear ploddy music, you know. It's an old wives' tale."

But J.J. *did* hear it. He heard a concertina, then two concertinas. He recognized the tunes. Two jigs that he had very recently learned. He recognized the playing as well. He had been hearing it all his life.

The charms of Tír na n'Óg abruptly lost their grip. He turned and began to walk purposefully through the trees, back the way they had come.

Aengus hurried after him, still carrying the dog. "Where are you going?"

"Home."

"Don't be a fool, J.J."

J.J. didn't stop. "I'm not such a fool as you think, Aengus Óg. They're still there. I can hear them. My mother and my sister, playing their concertinas."

He was out of the trees now and striding, nearly running, up the rocky slope toward the ring fort.

"J.J.! Wait!"

J.J. ignored him. Aengus had already tricked him into staying and would probably try to do it again.

"You belong here, J.J.," he was calling now. But J.J. knew where he belonged, and he wasn't going to be tricked again. The only thing that would stop him now was if Aengus turned him into a tortoise. Let him. He didn't care. He was going home.

But Aengus's next words did, in fact, stop him in his tracks.

"Take Bran with you!"

J.J. waited on the hillside for Aengus to catch up. Of course he would take Bran. He was surprised he hadn't thought of it himself. He wished he didn't have to do it, but there was no other way to end her misery. If Father Doherty hadn't stopped her, she would already have ended it herself.

Father Doherty. J.J. was suddenly less enthusiastic about going through the souterrain wall. He looked at Aengus.

"The priest," he said. "I suppose there'll be, you know, remains."

"Oh, yes," said Aengus. "Phew. Nasty."

J.J. was uncertain again. Already the lure of Tír na n'Óg was beginning to reassert itself. But for reasons known only to himself, Aengus Óg relented.

"No. He's gone, J.J. It's taken care of."

"How do you know?"

"Someone found him. They took him away. What was left of him."

"But how do you know?"

"We move easily between the worlds," said Aengus solemnly. "In the blink of an eye we are gone. In the same blink of the eye we are—"

"Yeah, yeah, yeah," said J.J. Despite all that had happened, J.J.'s heart warmed toward Aengus again.

"You'd want to watch yourself, you know. You're beginning to sound like a god."

Aengus roared with laughter. Together they continued up the hill to the rath, and there, between them, they maneuvered the distressed dog down into the souterrain. In its farthest corner, Aengus helped J.J. to balance her weight in his arms without losing his grip on the candle or the flute.

"Come back and play a tune with me sometime," he said.

"I will. I promise."

"You might forget."

"I won't. I'll try not to."

"Believe the things you remember, J.J. Even if they don't make sense."

It's not easy to hug a young man carrying a wolfhound, but Aengus Óg was a man, possibly even a god, of many talents. J.J. turned to face the wall. He would come again, he promised himself. But the gray dog, who had hunted Fionn Mac Cumhail's game from one end of the ancient world to the other, was leaving Tír na n'Óg forever.

"Good-bye, Bran," he whispered, and stepped forward.

THE MAPLE TREE

Trad

PART SIX

Ciaran and Marian were down at the GAA pitch, watching a camogie match. They had tried to persuade Helen to come with them, but she had resisted. She couldn't face the community that day. Whether or not Father Doherty was mentioned, his discovered remains would be haunting every eye that met hers.

When J.J. appeared in the kitchen doorway, her reaction was delayed. For an instant his presence there seemed like the most natural thing in the world, as though he had just walked up from the school bus. When the truth hit her, Helen went so weak at the knees that she had to hold on to the table for support as she stood up.

But J.J.'s behavior wasn't appropriate to the situation either. There was nothing in his manner to suggest that he had just returned from a month's unexplained absence. He plonked himself down in his usual chair and examined the flute that he was holding in his left hand.

"Where have you been?" Helen relinquished her grip on the table and hurried over to him.

J.J. flashed her a rapid, wild-eyed glance, then returned his attention to the flute.

"Nowhere," he said. "I dropped the cheese in to Anne Korff and then—" He broke off. There was a place in his mind where something was missing. He knew about the flute he was holding, but he couldn't remember where it had come from. "It used to have a ring across the middle where one end of it was older than the other," he said. "I can't see it now."

"J.J. . . . " Helen didn't know what to say. He looked exactly as he had when she last saw him, but he wasn't the same. He must know how worried they had been. Surely he would tell her?

"It was your grandfather's," said J.J. "His name is on it. Look. John Joseph Liddy."

"Where did you find it?"

"It must have been in the souterrain," said J.J.

"In the souterrain? What were you doing in there?"

The only response J.J. made was to open his right

hand, which, until then, had been clutched tight around something unseen. It was full of black dust, which trickled out between his fingers onto the worn flagstones.

"It's Bran," he said.

Helen's heart sank. Whatever had happened to J.J. had twisted his mind.

"It's not bran, love," she said gently.

"Not that kind of bran," said J.J. "It's a dog."

But even as he said the words, they made no sense to him. There were things bobbing around in that vacant place; words and images that didn't add up to anything. They frightened him. He wiped his hand on his jeans and scrubbed at the dust on the floor with his toe.

Helen was treading carefully, unsure how to deal with J.J.'s obvious disturbance. She resorted to the usual comfort.

"Come on. Take off your jacket there, and I'll make a fresh pot of tea."

He allowed her to help him take it off, moving the flute carefully from one hand to the other. As Helen hung the jacket up behind the door, she noticed that it was unusually bulky. All the outside pockets were bulging with something soft. Surreptitiously she slipped her hand into one of them. What she found there did nothing to reassure her fears about her son's state of mind. The pocket, and all the others as well, was stuffed to bursting with odd socks.

Helen turned, unsure whether to ask J.J. about them. He was just raising the flute to his lips and, after a few practice blows, he began to play a tune. Helen stood and listened. She didn't know the tune, but the exquisite tone of the old instrument seemed familiar to her, as though the memory of it had been passed down to her through her mother's blood.

"It's beautiful, J.J.," she said when he had finished.

"What's the name of it?" he asked.

"I've no idea. I never heard it before. Where did you learn it?"

"I don't know," said J.J. But he could hear it in his head, played by fiddles and flutes and a bodhrán, and he could see people dancing. "Are we having a céilí tonight?"

"No," said Helen. "I called it off."

"Why?"

"Because you weren't here."

"But I am here. Call it back on again."

"Is that what you want?" said Helen.

"Why wouldn't I?" said J.J.

Helen thought about it. Why not? A céilí could be just what J.J. needed. Hadn't the great Joe Cooley himself once said, "'Tis the only music that brings people to their senses"? Her heart warmed to the idea, and her concern for J.J. diminished. He was back, that was what mattered. In time he would feel able to explain where he had been, but in the meantime, Father Doherty or no Father Doherty, the Liddys would celebrate J.J.'s return.

But there were other things to be taken care of.

"We will have a céilí," said Helen. "But first we have to let the police know that you're back."

"The police?" said J.J. "Why on earth would you want to tell the police?"

It was only then that J.J. discovered the truth about how long he had been away.

WELCOME HOME

Trad

The new policeman had just reported for duty when Sergeant Early received the phone call from Helen Liddy. It was the second piece of good news to have arrived that day. A few hours earlier Séadna Tobín, the chemist, had turned up in the village. He was most apologetic for having wasted the Gardai's time and assured everyone that it wouldn't happen again. Under pressure, he confessed that he had been off on the tear with his fiddle. It was a weakness of his, he said. He intended, for the time being at least, to padlock the fiddle in a trunk and give his wife sole custody of the key.

"Both keys," he added, as an afterthought.

Now they'd found the Liddy boy as well, that just left Anne Korff and Thomas O'Neill. With a bit of luck they would soon turn up as well.

Saturday was a busy night for the police in Gort. Sergeant Early would have liked to go himself to visit the Liddys, but he was needed in the station. He would rather have sent anyone other than O'Dwyer, but he was, he had to admit, faced with no alternative. The other members of the force were already away on calls, and Garda Treacy, who ought to have been there, had failed to turn up.

"His car is there," said Larry. "His dog is in it, but he isn't."

"I didn't know he had a dog," said the sergeant. "You'll have to visit the Liddys on your own, so. But tread carefully, you hear? There's no knowing what that boy might have been through."

Marian and Ciaran arrived soon after Helen had spoken to Sergeant Early. They were as surprised and delighted, and soon as concerned, as Helen was. J.J. had been badly shocked to learn that he had been away for a month, but as time went on and some kind of semblance of family normality began to return, he relaxed and appeared to be recovering well. Marian, in her usual perceptive way, honed in on the best method of keeping him focused on the present. She told him all the latest gossip from the village, filling him in on the disappearances first, then going on to the more humdrum stuff like the hurling results, the breakups and makeups, the appearance of white donkeys, and associated trivia. Neither she nor the others mentioned the discovery of the body in the souterrain. There would be time enough for that in the future.

When Helen brought the policeman into the kitchen, J.J. recognized him. A name was on the point of escaping from his lips when some strong instinct urged him to keep them closed. Before he could get a grip on them, the name and the face had both slithered away again, back into the place where the whole of his lost month was hiding.

Marian was out in the hall, phoning every musician and dancer in the county. The policeman sat opposite J.J. at the table, and Helen and Ciaran, after hovering uncertainly for a minute or two, settled into the armchairs on either side of the range.

But the interview was remarkably brief. J.J. told the policeman that he could remember nothing. Three or four questions later, there had been no progress beyond that basic but comprehensive stumbling block. J.J. didn't mention the flute and, on reflection, Helen decided that she wouldn't either. If the forensics people had overlooked it during their examination of the souterrain, that was their problem. She had no desire to further incriminate her grandfather.

Garda O'Dwyer felt that there was probably a way of dealing with situations like this, but if he'd ever learned about them, he'd already forgotten. He suggested that a visit to their GP would do J.J. no harm, and if that turned up no causes for the amnesia they might consider arranging an appointment with a counselor. Helen and Ciaran agreed readily.

"Right, so," said the new policeman. "It's good to see the lad back home again, anyway. If there's anything else we can do, let us know."

"Will you have a cup of tea before you go?" said Helen.

"I won't, thanks all the same."

"We heard on the grapevine that you're a great fiddle player."

"Ah, well. I wouldn't say great."

Helen stood up and took J.J.'s fiddle down from the wall. "Did you ever see a fiddle like this one?"

J.J. was embarrassed. Helen always did this: showed off his fiddle to anyone who might know anything about them at all. They always agreed that it was a wonderful instrument, but then what else could they say?

The policeman took the fiddle and gazed at it.

Gradually, a fond smile appeared on his face. J.J. watched him. Memories were darting around just beneath the surface of his consciousness, but they were quick and slippery, like little fish, and he couldn't quite get a grip on them.

"I did, once," said Garda O'Dwyer, handing the fiddle back to Helen. She took it back, disappointed that he showed no inclination to play it.

"We have a céilí here tonight," she said.

"A céilí," said O'Dwyer. "Very good."

"You'd be more than welcome to come."

"That's very kind of you, but I'm on duty. And when I'm finished for the night, I shall more than likely go home."

"Well," said Helen, a little crestfallen, "there'll be another one next month."

"I doubt if I'll be here then." O'Dwyer stood up and moved toward the door. "Good-bye, J.J.," he said. "Perhaps we'll meet again. Some other time."

J.J. said nothing as the policeman left. The memories were jumping now, like the same little fish rising after flies. But he still couldn't see them clearly.

"Strange character," said Helen.

"Certainly is," said Ciaran. "Did you see his face when you showed him the fiddle?"

"I wouldn't mind that so much," said Helen. "But how could you take a policeman seriously when he's wearing odd socks?"

J.J. stared at the door. That was it. That was the net that brought the memories, twisting and shimmering, up to where he could see them. And here, in a world with a time scale, they fitted themselves, quickly and neatly, into a pattern that he hadn't seen before.

He ran to the door and out into the yard. The policeman was walking briskly down the drive, barely visible in the approaching night. J.J. ran to the gate and called out after him. The policeman stopped and waited. When J.J. caught up with him, he said, "What did you just call me?"

"Granddad," said J.J.

"Oh," said the policeman. "That's all right then. It sounded a lot like 'Aengus' to me."

"Would I call you that?" said J.J., falling happily into step beside his fairy grandfather.

"No," said Aengus. "You'd know better. Unlike some people."

They walked on a bit farther, delighted to be in each other's company again so soon.

"Where did you leave your car?" said J.J.

"In a ditch," said Aengus. "I still can't understand

why you people think two cars can pass each other on these roads."

"They can," said J.J. "It's ploddy magic. Where are you going now?"

"Home," said Aengus. "I've had enough of indulging my fantasies for at least another century or two. Besides, the job's done, isn't it? The leak is mended."

"And did it help?" said J.J. "Being a policeman?"

"Not remotely," said Aengus. "I can't imagine why I ever thought it would."

They walked on in agreeable silence for a bit farther, then Aengus went on, "Will you come for a visit?"

"I'll be there in no time," said J.J. "But I'd better wait awhile until things settle down here."

"As long as you don't forget," said Aengus.

"I won't," said J.J. "But you will. A couple of dances and you'll have forgotten I ever existed."

"Maybe three," said Aengus.

"Should I tell Mum, do you think?" said J.J.

"Best not to. She wouldn't believe you, and if she did it would be worse. You people seem to have difficulty with the notion of having parents who are younger than you."

"I suppose so," said J.J.

Helen was calling him from the gate.

"I'd better go back. Will you do one thing before you go home?"

"What thing?"

"Turn that white donkey back into Thomas O'Neill?"

"No bother," said Aengus Óg.

He walked away down the road, and it appeared to J.J. that he vanished from his sight just a fraction before the darkness swallowed him up. J.J. was to meet up with him again, of course, and all the others in Tír na n'Óg as well. But neither the new policeman nor Anne Korff were ever seen in Kinvara again.

GRANDFATHER'S PET

Trad

The céilí, everyone agreed, was the best ever. There were those who didn't come and would never come again because of what they believed had happened to Father Doherty, but they were few and far between. Three of the four missing people had turned up alive and well, and everyone was sure that Anne Korff would soon be back again, too, with her little dog at her heels. The relief of the whole district was evident in the smiling faces of the musicians and the flying feet of the dancers.

Helen was astonished by J.J. Something had happened to his playing while he'd been away. He leaned on the bow, full of flair and confidence, and his rhythm was electric. She had never heard anyone, past or present, play with such lift and such elegance.

The old fiddle, beneath his deft fingers, sang out so beautifully that she wondered whether even a Stradivarius could sound better.

But the strangest thing of all about J.J.'s playing was the new tunes. About halfway through the evening, Helen got up to stretch her legs. The dancers relaxed, assuming that there was going to be a break, and were congregating around the bar, when J.J. did a thing he had never done before. He began to play a tune on his own.

Helen had turned around to go and join in with him before she realized that she didn't know the tune. Nor did she know the one that followed it, nor the one after that. Phil didn't know them either, and nor did Marian or any of the other musicians who had come to celebrate with the Liddys that night. But J.J. didn't appear to need any support. The rich tones of his grandfather's fiddle filled the barn and set the feet of the dancers moving to a rhythm that wasn't quite like any they'd come across before. They found a new freedom in the music; they broke out of their sets and improvised alone or in pairs, their limbs and their hearts light and free.

J.J.'s cheek rested lightly on the chin rest. His eyes gazed dreamily into the middle distance, and his lips formed an unself-conscious smile. He played like a boy who was born to play for dancing; like a boy who had heard the fairy music; like a boy who was soon to mature into one of the greatest traditional musicians Ireland had ever known.

The other players listened, mesmerized by the performance. Only J.J. knew that he wasn't playing alone. Only he could hear the faint strains of Aengus's fiddle and Devaney's bodhrán leaking through from the copse of chiming maples in Tír na n'Óg, leading him through the beautiful set of reels. When the last of them was over, he was amazed to find himself in the barn and even more amazed by the applause that followed his playing. He grinned bashfully and hugged the fiddle to his chest.

"Where did you learn those tunes?" said Helen, resuming her seat beside him. J.J. had already decided to stick to the lost memory story.

"I don't know," he said.

"You'll have to teach them to me," said Helen. She finished her drink, picked up the concertina, and asked the dancers to get ready for the Plain Set. "Any suggestions?" she asked J.J.

"What about 'Devaney's Goat'?"

"Oh, lovely," said Helen. "We haven't played that in ages. What'll we put with it?"

J.J. suggested another tune, one that he knew but couldn't remember too well. Helen agreed and, as soon as the dancers had gotten back into their sets, tore into "Devaney's Goat." J.J. romped through it happily, but when Helen changed to the second tune, he dropped out for a few bars, listening. In a flash the tune came back to him. It was a great tune. How could he have forgotten it?

Through the leak he heard a hesitation similar to his own, then the joyful return of the fiddle and bodhrán as Aengus and Devaney remembered it as well. J.J. could almost see the smiles on their faces. He had a feeling that this might not be the last time they joined in with the Liddys on céilí night.

"Mum," he said to Helen when the tunes came to an end, "have you noticed that there seems to be more time than there used to be?"

"I certainly have," said Helen. "Everyone has. It's amazing."

J.J. smiled. "That was my birthday present to you," he said. "You asked for time, and I bought it for you."

"Really?" said Helen. She regarded J.J. carefully and decided to treat this particular eccentricity as a joke.

"Really," said J.J. "And I just paid for it."

"Did you?" said Helen. "And how much was it?"

"Not much," said J.J. "Not much at all. You'd be amazed at what you can buy these days for 'Dowd's Number Nine.'"

DOWD'S NUMBER
NINE

Trad

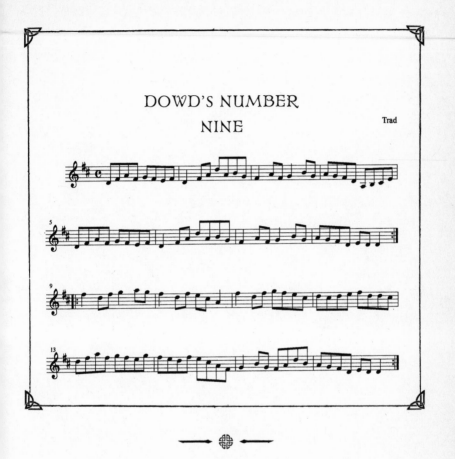

AUTHOR'S NOTE

A few years ago a special auction was held in Kinvara to raise money for a new community center. It was an "Auction of Promises" so, instead of donating items to be sold, local people offered promises related to their skills; anything from computer lessons to music lessons, decorating to car maintenance. I was asked if I would give a promise to put someone's name in my next book, and the successful bidder on the night was a local publisher of beautiful maps and guidebooks relating to the area.

It was some time before I got around to writing the next book, and in the meantime I met the publisher at a music session in the Auld Plaid Shawl. We had a discussion, which only just fell short of an argument, about the nature of the promise. In my opinion I was only required to use her name for a character of my choice, but she was convinced that I was under obligation to write a book which actually contained her. Afterwards I was determined to stick to my guns and use her name only, but over the next few weeks and months I realized that she had unwittingly planted the seed of an idea, which fused with other ideas already knocking around in my head and eventually became *The New Policeman*.

The name of the publisher is Anne Korff and if you have read this far, you have already met her. Apart from a couple of mentions of actual legendary musicians, such as Micho Russell, Paddy Fahy, etc., there are only two other real people in the book. They are Séadna Tobín, Kinvara's fiddle-playing pharmacist, and Mary Green, landlady of Green's pub.

I would like to thank Máire O'Keeffe for her invaluable help with the tunes.

Kate Thompson, 2005

To all the players, past and present, whose love of this music has kept it alive.

Thanks for the tunes.

The tunes in this book have been gathered from various sources. Most of them I have learned over the last few years from other musicians, and these I have transcribed from memory. Others have been taken from a variety of published sources, including *O'Neill's Dance Music of Ireland* and Breandán Breathnach's excellent series, *Ceol Rince na hÉireann*. As far as I have been able to ascertain, all the tunes I have used (with the exception of three) are traditional and the composers are unknown.

There are many different methods of transcribing Irish traditional music and the one I have chosen to use will not please everyone. However, I hope it will give easy access to the tunes for anyone interested in playing them. For anyone new to Irish music who would like to explore further, the best way to learn is to find a good teacher. If that isn't possible, there are many excellent primers available. For fiddle I would recommend *The Irish Fiddle Book*, by Matt Crannitch.

GLOSSARY

Aengus Óg (A-ehn-gus Ohg)—Celtic god of love, youth, and beauty.

Amadán (AHM-uh-daw*n, AHM-uh-don)—Fool, idiot.

Bodhrán (bo-rahn, bow-rawn)—A traditional Irish drum made from goatskin.

Burren (taken from the Irish word *Boireann*)—Great limestone barrier that spans the landscape of Ireland's County Clare.

Camogie (cam-ohg-ee)—The women's version of hurling, which is a very old and very fast ball game.

Céilí (KAY-lee, KAY*-li-he)—A dance.

Ciaran (KEER-ahn, KEE a rahn)—Ciaran Byrne, J.J. Liddy's father.

Craic (CRACK)—Fun

Dagda, the (Dah dah, däg'du, dahg-dah)—Son of the goddess **Danu** and father of Aengus Óg, the Dagda is referred to as *The Good God*. He was the ruler and protector of the Tuatha de Danaan.

Diarmuid (deer + mid)—Raised by Aengus Óg, Diarmuid was a warrior of the Fianna who had a magic love mark on his head. Any woman to see the mark would instantly fall in love with him, including Gráinne, the bride of Fionn mac Cumhail who ran away with Diarmuid.

Fianna (fee + ina, Fee'awn'a, fee-anna, FEEN-oh)—Legendary army of Irish warriors who served the High King of Ireland.

Fionn mac Cumhail (fin, FYOON, Fee'nn / McCool)—The most heroic and celebrated leader of the Fianna.

Fleadh (Flaa, Flah)—A festival. A competition for Irish traditional music.

GAA—Gaelic Athletic Association. The governing body of Irish sports (hurling and Gaelic football).

Garda (GAHR-duh, gar'-da, GAR-dah, GORR-doh, gorda)—Irish policeman.

Gardai (gar-DEE, GORR-DEE, gawr-dhee)—Plural form of policeman.

Garda Síochána (shee-oh-CAHN-nah, shee-uch-awna)—Ireland's national police force.

Gráinne (GRAWNyeah, grawn'-ya)—The bride of Fionn mac Cumhail, Gráinne fell in love with Diarmuid and cast a spell to persuade him to betray Fionn mac Cumhail and run away with her.

Hornpipe—A dance tune in common time but with a distinctly different rhythm from a reel.

Hundredth monkey—A scientific experiment showed that when a certain number of monkeys learned a new skill, the entire species learned it, even though most of them had never seen the skill used.

Jig—A dance tune in 6/8 time. A slip jig is in 9/8 time.

Merrows (from Gaelic murúch, or murrough)—Merpeople.

Oisín (oh'-sheen, uh-sheen)—Son of Fionn mac Cumhail, Oisín was a poet and warrior of the Fianna who went to live in Tír na n'Óg for what seemed to him three years. When he attempted to return to his homeland he discovered that three hundred years had actually passed.

Púka (pooka, phooka)—A mythical creature that appears in the form of a goat.

Rath (rah, rath)—Fairy fort or ring.
Reel—A dance tune in common time.

Sean nós (shan nohs)—Literally "old style." There are sean nós forms of singing and of dancing.
Set dance—A dance with eight people, which has a number of different parts.
Sidhe (she, shee)—An old word, literally meaning a hill, for the fairy folk.
Souterrain—An underground chamber or series of chambers, commonly found in ancient Irish ring forts.

Tír na n'Óg (teer na nogue, Tier nah Nohg)—The Land of Eternal Youth.

Tuatha de Danaan (TOO 'ha dA Dah n'n, Too watha day danan)—Literally meaning, *People of the Goddess Danu*, the Tuatha de Danaan were immortal beings who possessed magical abilities and excelled at art, poetry, music, and warfare. They were pushed out of their homeland and relegated to the sidhe, where they remained forever young

BIBLIOGRAPHY

Gregory, Lady Augusta. *Gods and Fighting Men.* 1904. Reprint, Whitefish, Montana: Kessinger Publishing Co., 2004.

—*Cuchulain of Muirthemne.* 1902. Reprint, Mineola, New York: Dover Publications, 2001.

—*Visions and Beliefs in the West of Ireland.* 1920. Reprint, Buckinghamshire, United Kingdom: Colin Smythe Ltd., 1976.

Stephens, James. *Irish Fairy Tales.* 1920. Reprint, Milton Keynes, United Kingdom: Lightning Source U.K. Ltd., 2004.

Wilde, Lady Jane Francesca. *Ancient Legends, Mystic Charms, and Superstitions of Ireland.* 1887. Reprint, New York: Lemma Publishing Corporation, 1973.